Brett Wilson and Coronado's Door

John V. Suter

CrossLink Publishing
RAPID CITY, SD

Suter/CrossLink Publishing
1601 Mt Rushmore Rd. Ste 3288
Rapid City, SD 57701
www.CrossLinkPublishing.com

Ordering Information:
Quantity sales. Special discounts are available on quantity purchases by corporations, associations, and others. For details, contact the "Special Sales Department" at the address above.

Brett Wilson and Coronado's Door/John V. Suter. —1st ed.
ISBN 978-1-63357-357-4
Library of Congress Control Number 2020945903

To Rebecca, Rory, and Garrett.
They always make the adventure.

Contents

Chapter 1: The Disappearance 1

Chapter 2: Unexpected Gift 13

Chapter 3: Searching for Answers 21

Chapter 4: Meeting of the Minds 27

Chapter 5: The Great Escape 37

Chapter 6: Finding Anomalies 43

Chapter 7: Trapped 51

Chapter 8: Go West 57

Chapter 9: Esteban's Trail 65

Chapter 10: Coronado's Ghost 79

Chapter 11: Shining City on the Hill 91

Chapter 12: The Noble Sentry 103

Chapter 13: The Return 111

About the Author 115

References 117

CHAPTER 1

The Disappearance

It is a clear night out in the canyons of New Mexico. Rock Wilson and his team of scientists have arrived in Thoreau a few days before to begin exploring the canyons to the northwest. Brett, his eleven-year-old daughter, has enjoyed the days looking at the crimson and orange canyon walls, trying to figure out what types of rocks they are and when they formed. She always has her rock hammer looped in her belt, ready for action, and in the sandstones of the southwest it could mean busting a rock open and finding a unique fossil. She has cracked at least one hundred stones during the day, and luckily, she has located a few leaves embedded in the coarse sedimentary rock.

Now she is sitting on top of a ledge, looking out at the night sky. The stars are twinkling brightly against the purple pool of space above her. She holds the leaf fossils in her hands, feeling the roughness of the sand grains in her fingers. A smile crosses her face because of the productive day out in the field. Her day has been successful, but that isn't the only success. Her dad's team has used a device they designed to locate magnetic abnormalities in the earth. They have carried it down into every canyon for the last week without much luck, but today things have changed. The magnetoscope has worked, and now not only is Brett excited for her venture into paleontology, but she is excited because tomorrow the team will finally find a treasure that no one has seen in a very long time: one of the Seven Cities of Gold.

1

Brett hears the crackling of static coming from a table-like protrusion of rock that extends out over the cliff. She can see a small light moving, and this makes her curious. Brett stands up, brushing the grains of sand from her pants. She can hear the distinct sounds of a crowd cheering through the static. She walks slowly toward the source of the static with her hands deep in her pockets, and with each step she can see that her father is doing one of his favorite things: he is listening to a baseball game.

"How's the game? she asks.

Rock looks up at her with a smile on his face, "We are out here and the Royals are playing. W hat could be better?"

Brett smiles. They have been going on these field studies for years, and they always listen to a game the night before a discovery. This is something Brett truly enjoys—the buildup and time spent sitting with her dad as they talk about its importance while a Royals game plays in the background.

Brett kicks a yellowish- orange rock from the cliff and watches it bounce off the canyon walls lit up by the moonlight until it is lost in the darkness. "I didn't think you' d be in bed by now ," Rock says. "I know you' re ready for some conversation and a game. A m I right ?

Brett looks away from the valley below and smiles at her dad. "Always." The announcer sputters, "Alex Gordon up with two outs here in the seventh."

Brett brushes her long sandy-blonde hair from her face and sits down. She straightens out her brown cargo pants and begins playing with the laces on her boots. "I thought *you* would be a little more jubilant, considering we are almost to the city of gold."

"And I thought hiking all day out here would tire you out," Rock laughs. "I knew that wouldn't happen."

"I'm excited! " Brett says a little too jubilantly as her voice echoes off the rocks. Her dad never shows excitement in words or expression, and this always makes her feel silly when her voice echoes off canyon walls.

"Let's just sit here in the moonlight and catch the last few innings of the game together, " Rock says.

"Aren't you at least a little bit excited?" Brett asks.

"Yes. I'm excited," he replies. "We are on the verge of finding something that has remained hidden for hundreds of years."

"Then why are we sitting here under the full moon listening to a baseball game?"

A warm wind blows over the clifftops as the two look at each other. Brett watches as her dad runs his hands through his hair again and pulls at the white T-shirt he is wearing. He points down into the canyon. "Down there lies the entrance to one of the seven lost cities of gold."

Brett follows her father's hand toward the weathered orange walls gleaming in the moonlight. He is smiling broadly. "Down there is what I have been searching for all these years."

"And you are *this* close," she says, pinching her thumb and forefinger together to indicate a smidgen .

"*This* close," he agrees .

"Why are we up here when the city is down there?" Brett asks. "And why are we wasting time listening to a baseball game when we could be sleeping in the City of Gold tonight?"

Brett is confused by what is happening. They are sitting here doing nothing, and now Rock leans back and smiles toward the stars. She doesn't quite understand, and he looks at her like he doesn't want to hurt her feelings. She doesn't like that look. That is the look he always gives before he corrects her. "There is more to it than just walking into that canyon and entering the City of Gold."

"Someone else would have found it if it were that easy," Brett answers.

"Precisely," Rock agrees.

"Then how do you know when you can enter?"

Rock pats her on the shoulder. "I think my daughter can figure that one out on her own."

She looks out at the canyon below . "That's why we've been taking all of these electromagnetic readings and correlating them with the past anomalies."

Rock nods while he takes out a worn and tattered leather field journal. He hands her the book, and she opens it with care. Some of the pages are yellowed and brittle, and she turns the pages very carefully. "Is t here a specific time and place when you can access the city?"

Rock smiles broadly as his daughter begins to piece the puzzle together. He feels that she is just as worthy of this journey—this discovery—as he is, and he is pleased that he brought her.

Brett looks up into Rock's smiling face. She knows that smile. It is the smile that he puts on when he gives her a problem that he knows the answer to but will not tell her. Just like when she asks him, "What kind of rock is this?" and he always replies, "What does the rock say to you?" She has learned very quickly that he will not give her answers, and out here in this canyon, he is doing the same thing.

"Tomorrow is the day," she says.

"Tomorrow is the day," Rock replies. "July nin th."

"July nin th," she answers.

"Willie Wilson's birthday. Some coincidence."

"Willie Wilson?" she asks.

"The best center fielder the Royals ever had," he replies.

"Of course he is, and the date we can go in is on his birthday."

"Funny, huh?"

"So, we are sitting here enjoying a game, waiting for Willie Wilson's birthday."

"Yes. M y daughter and I camping under the stars, enjoying a Royals baseball game." He smiles. "Our discovery can wait a few more hours. Happy Birthday, Willie."

"What about everyone else?" Brett asks.

Rock holds his hand out, and Brett places the book back in his hand. He puts the book back into the pouch under his shirt and pats it with his hand. "They don't truly know what we're here to find. They believe we are using electromagnetics to find valuable ore deposits." Brett stares at him in disbelief. Dr. Mies is her dad's best friend. They have worked together for at least ten years, and they have always been discussing scientific research what they've been doing. Dr. Mies is a genuine and caring man. He has always been pleasant to Brett when she hangs out at the college.

Creighton Sims, on the other hand, has never been good to her. He always questions why an eleven-year-old girl should be allowed in the geologic offices of Montlake College. He thinks the school is prestigious and should not pander to the whims of a professor who wants his daughter exposed to higher-order thinking.

The other scientists in the party are mostly just names to Brett. She has never really had any interactions with them. Dr. Emily Brown is a female who studies rocks. That is abnormal, but she is firm with the men in the group. She is fierce in her ideas, and Brett likes that about her. Charlie Spain is a graduate assistant who is always curious and wanting to know more.

"You never showed them the book?" she asks.

"Never," he says. "I never will, either. All the secrets of the quest are in the book, and it must be protected." Rock laughs and places his hand on his daughter's shoulder again. "Well, maybe Zach can be trusted."

The announcer screams over the receiver, "Here's the pitch by Boyd. Gordon swings, and there's a long drive to deep center. Jones going back. He's going to run out of room. It's a home run!" Rock claps and holds his hands up over his head. The night couldn't be any better. The Royals are winning, Rock and his daughter are enjoying a moonlit night in New Mexico, and tomorrow they will be walking into the city of Cibola.

*****

It is a cloudless morning when Brett climbs out of her tent. She wipes the sleep out of her eyes and looks around the campsite. Brett looks over at Dr. Mies as he fiddles with the dials on a machine. There is already sweat forming in beads on his bald head. The machine emits a squawk and ping. Dr. Mies adjusts the dials, and a slow hum begins transmitting from the device.

Dr. Mies looks up, and he nods to Brett. "Today is the day!" he says. "Today, we find out if our calculations are accurate." He walks over to Brett and points toward Rock. Rock is standing at the edge of the cliff, drinking the last bit of his coffee. "I don't think he slept much last night," Dr. Mies says.

Brett smiles. "I don't think many of us slept that much," Brett replies.

"Being this close to finding something so extraordinary can cause a lack of sleep."

Brett looks at Dr. Mies with her brow furrowed. *Does he know?* Her father has told her last night that the two of them are the only ones who kno w about the city. Maybe she ha s misunderstood what her father told her.

Dr. Mies leans in close to her ear. "I know what we are after."

Brett cannot believe it, but Dr. Mies is her father's best friend, so obviously, he knows the secret.

Brett looks over the busy camp. Dr. Sims is standing with his arms crossed, staring at Rock. Dr. Mies follows her gaze. "That is the reason for the secrecy," he says in a low voice. "Rock doesn't trust that guy."

Brett watches Dr. Sims. He is well dressed, unlike Dr. Mies and Rock Wilson. Dr. Sims is wearing a pair of pressed brown slacks and a button-down white shirt which is starched. Sim's elegant style differs significantly from how most geologists dress in the field, but Dr. Sims is a dainty man and has contempt for dirt. He wears a pair of round glasses that give his eyes an oversized look.

"We don't want him knowing about Cibola," Dr. Mies says.

Brett nods her head as she watches Dr. Sims. "I agree," she replies.

Rock Wilson dumps the coffee from his cup and checks his watch. It is seven, and the sun is starting to rise in the east. The first rays of sunlight spray the orange rock with spatters of yellowish light. Rock turns and yells, "Time to move out!" He grabs his worn leather bag and throws it over his shoulder. He walks over to Brett and Dr. Mies, a nd Rock grabs Brett by the shoulder. He kneels so his face is directly in front of hers. He glares at her sternly, but he winks at her with his bright-blue eyes shining like beacons in the morning glow. A smile spreads across his tanned face. "You ready?" he asks. Brett smiles back and nods.

Rock looks up at Dr. Mies and winks. "Your electroscope tuned in?" he asks. Dr. Mies shows him the instrument, and it emits a steady hum.

Rock turns to the others. Emily Brown and Charlie walk up, both carrying their packs. "Ready?" Charlie asks . Rock looks questioningly at Emily.

"All the sample containers are in my pack, " she confirms.

"All right, let' s begin our descent into the rugged canyon," Rock says. "Watch your step."

"Watch *your* step, Dr. Wilson," Emily replies. Rock laughs as Emily walks by him, but she gives him a penetrating glare that says, *You're the old man of the group, and you might fall and break a hip.* He looks down at Brett with a *Can you believe that?* look on his face. *I was just trying to be nice.*

Brett stares at Dr. Brown as she begins climbing down the narrow rock ledge that leads into the deep, craggy canyon below. "I think she can handle it," Brett says.

Rock pats her on the shoulder. "I know she can handle herself. She is one of the most rugged, sure-footed geologists I've met. If I'm ever in a difficult situation, I would want her on the team."

Dr. Mies walks by, laughing. "I wonder what he says about me when I'm not around."

Rock glares at him. "I say I'm glad you're not around."

Dr. Mies places his wide-brimmed hat on his head and walks out onto the ledge. He disappears down the slope.

Rock and Brett are standing at the top, looking down the ledge. Emily is the first, moving gently down the treacherous path. Behind her is Charlie, followed by Dr. Mies. Rock and Brett watch them with apprehension as the others cautiously place each foot on the rocky ledge. The crunch of gravel causes Brett to turn. Standing behind her is Creighton Sims. He wipes the sweat from his glasses as he looks over the edge. "A trek like this is not suitable for a little girl," he says. "So much danger out here in this harsh environment. One slip, and your little life ends quite quickly."

"Leave her alone!" Rock says.

"I'm sorry," he replies. "I was just trying to look out for the little girl."

"She doesn't need you looking out for her," Rock says sternly.

"It seems she needs someone," he responds. "Look at this place."

"I will be fine!" Brett yells.

Sims places the glasses back on his head and smirks. He looks down the pathway toward the valley and begins the downward trek into the abyss. Rock watches him walk gingerly over the rocks. As he moves farther down the path, Rock grabs his daughter and hugs her. "This is it."

Brett smiles and whispers, "Let's find Cibola." She walks down the ledge first, followed by her father.

The pathway is narrow, and the rocks are loose under her feet. Brett walks cautiously, making sure her feet are on something substantial before she puts her full weight down. The sun is hidden behind the vertical rock wall as they descend.

After what seems like hours, the group is finally on the canyon floor. The sun has not risen high enough into the sky to light the bottom where the group now finds themselves. They are in shadows as they start moving northwest with the tall orange rocks hovering over them. Dr. Mies is leading the group, with the magnetoscope held out in front of him. He peers back at Rock as the transmitter vibrates violently in his hand. The two men talk in hurried, hushed voices as they look at the magnetoscope. The humming coming from the machine is getting more forceful the farther northwest they go. They are getting closer to the source of the anomaly.

Brett is observing all the layers of rock that are visible along the canyon walls. The colors of the exposed rock change from dark orange to a pebbly- grayish brown. She runs her dry fingers along the rock face as she walks by, and the rock is abrasive and filled with tiny sand grains. The distinct patterns in the stone give her the impression that it formed in a marine environment. The small undulations and fine grains of orange sand remind her of a beach. As she walks farther, she begins processing the data that she is seeing and feeling. Analyzing data is something that her dad has taught her throughout her life: "Observe and analyze." Those are his favorite words whenever the two of them are out on a trip like this one.

Dr. Brown increases her speed and walks beside Brett, watching her feel the rocks. She can see that Brett is thinking about the texture and structure of the rock. "It is impressive, isn't it?" Emily asks.

Brett jumps at the sudden sound of Emily's voice. She has been so focused on what she is observing and analyzing that she hasn't noticed Dr. Brown walking next to her. "What? Oh, yes." Brett responds.

"You have that same intense look that Dr. Wilson gets when he is trying to solve something."

"Like father, like daughter," Brett says.

"I believe you are right," Dr. Brown says. "I think it is wonderful that he brought you with him on this research trip."

"I like coming," Brett answers.

"I wish my father would have been as . . ."

The humming from the machine is becoming more violent in its intensity. Brett hears it clearly, and she is thirty yards behind Rock and Dr. Mies. They stop in their tracks and are looking up the valley, pointing. It appears that their mouths are hanging open as they stare northward up the canyon pathway. They are talking excitedly, and Dr. Mies looks down at the magnetoscope.

The sound coming from the machine is echoing harshly off the canyon walls. Dr. Brown begins walking forward. "I think they've found something." She starts walking briskly toward Rock. Dr. Sims and Charlie rush up to Brett as she stares at her father.

In the distance, she can see a shimmer through the valley. It looks like heat bands coming off an asphalt road on a hot summer day. She sees Rock and Dr. Mies start walking faster through the canyon toward the shimmering structure that pulses in the valley. She begins walking swiftly toward them. The intensity of the humming coming from the valley continues to grow. The sound is causing her ears to ring as she moves closer.

Brett looks up, and through the heat bands she can see the traces of a building silhouetted through the vibrant waves of heat in the air. The sunlight is glinting off the walls, and the rays reflect brightly off the surface in a bright-gold luster. Her heart is pounding against her ribcage. They have found it.

The humming has become amplified, and she covers her ears with her shaking hands. It is starting to make her eyes water and her ears burn. She looks away from the glowing golden city and struggles to find her father.

Rock looks back at his daughter as he continues toward the glowing city in front of him. His ears are aching as he gets closer to the source of the vibrant humming sound. He can see that she is looking up ahead of him. She has seen the city. A smile spreads across his face as he nears the city walls.

Brett watches her father move faster and faster through the heat bands. Suddenly the pitch of the humming changes. The frequency has become high pitched, and the whining sound almost sends her to her knees. She thrusts her hands over her aching ears. She gasps as the sound of the machine stops, and instantly her father and Dr. Mies have vanished.

*****

The state police arrive a few hours later. The uniformed officers scour every square inch of the desolate canyon, but they can't find a trace of Rock and Dr. Mies. The search goes on for a week without ever locating the two scientists.

Dr. Brown does not leave Brett's side during the search for her father. Brett is in shock from the loss of her father. She doesn't understand what is happening. She answers what seems like a million questions about what they were doing and what she saw. Dr. Brown reassures her that they will find her dad.

The reality, however, is they never fi nd Rock Wilson or Zachary Mies. They are gone! Brett makes a vow after all of her tears a re shed: Her father isn't dead! He is alive! She will find him!

CHAPTER 2

Unexpected Gift

The morning air is stale, and it feels like it is already one hundred degrees. A large thermometer built into a Coke bottle that is hanging on the side of the wood-paneled barn says that it is only 85°F. Eighty-five degrees at ten in the morning is still unseasonable for Tennessee at the beginning of August. A month has passed since the disappearance of her dad, and her tears and anger still return at night as she tries to sleep. The only refuge is taking care of the goats on her grandfather's farm. This gives her a few hours of joy before the waves of reality break over her and bring the pain of losing him back again and again.

Brett opens up the stall door and lets the Lamancha goats out into the field. She pats a large brown goat as she hurries out the door. There are ten of the earless goats trying to get through the opening. They bunch together, trying to be the first to eat the fresh green grass outside. "Hurry up, Alex," she says. "You're holding up the line."

Alex, the white goat, jumps in the air and darts out of the stall. The other goats follow her through the opening. Brett closes the wooden gate and walks outside. She pulls her wide-brimmed hat down to shield her eyes from the glaring sun. She watches the goats bounding around in the field, playing. It is terrific taking care of playful animals. It is great having something that she is interested in again.

After her father's disappearance, Brett has focused her time and energy solely on finding him. She reads up on electromagnetism, resonance, groundwater amplification, and any other topic that will help her locate her dad. Unfortunately, all her efforts have proven fruitless. She even begi ns questioning if she actually saw the shimmering city or if it was a false phenomenon, like a mirage in the desert. None of the other members of the group have witnessed the golden walls that she has seen. They have n't seen any of it. Maybe she has imagined the entire thing.

It has been a month since John "Rock" Wilson disappeared. A month of learning and pondering and guessing. It has been exhausting for her. She didn't think she would lose both parents by the time she was eleven, but here she is without either of them. Brett does not remember her mother. She looks at her pictures often and wonders what she was like, and she wishes she were here now. That would help her. She could comfort her. As of this moment, Brett has been a failure at figuring out what happened to her dad. She still believes that she will find the answer, but the harsh reality of failure and loneliness is smothering her.

Brett walks across the field toward the gate. Alex runs toward her, bleating loudly. Brett stops and turns. "What is it, girl?" The goat pushes her head into Brett's hand. Brett pets her head and neck. "I will be back in a little while," she says.

Brett opens the latch and closes it behind her. Alex bleats loudly. Brett turns around. "I will be back at noon to feed you," she says. Brett walks up the hill toward the white farmhouse that sits amid three tall pecan trees.

She climbs up the steps toward the front door. She opens the screen door and peers inside. "Grandpa!" she yells. "I'm going over to Montlake to see Natalie." Standing motionless, she is listening for Grandpa Jake to answer. She starts to close the door but hears something. It is the heavy footfalls of Grandpa Jake coming from the upstairs. "What's that?" he asks.

"I'm heading over to Montlake to see Natalie."

Grandpa Jake is a short, portly man with white sideburns and long white hair. His tan, calloused hands grip the straps of his faded overalls. Grandpa Jake looks like your typical old farmer, and he has taught Brett all about tending to goats. The goats have become an escape for her. When she is with them, she doesn't think about the loss of her dad that much.

Grandpa Jake doesn't talk about his son either. He honestly believes the flimsy rationale of the state police of New Mexico and the authorities at Montlake College: Rock Wilson died accidentally. He believes that Brett needs to move on, and he tries to help her by giving her another purpose. The goats are that purpose.

"Going over to Montlake?"

"Yes, sir," she replies.

"Did you get the animals taken care of?"

"Yes, sir," she says. "Clipped their hooves and let them out."

"All right," Grandpa Jake says. "I'll have a turkey sandwich ready for you when you get back."

Grandpa Jake knows that when Brett visits Montlake College, she is always back by noon. She always goes over at ten, and she is back by lunch, and Grandpa Jake has a delectable sandwich waiting when she returns. "Okay, Grandpa, see you in a bit," she says.

Brett closes the door and jumps down off the porch. What Grandpa Jake doesn't know is that she is continuing to search for her father. Natalie helps sometimes, but today she is on her own.

Brett races around the house. She jumps on her bike that is sitting beside the faded cellar door. She pushes off and pedals quickly, gaining speed as she glides down the slope toward the road. The gravel crunches under the tires as she speeds down the driveway. It generally takes about five minutes for Brett to bike over to the campus at Montlake.

She pedals faster down the main road lined with Bradford pear trees. They have lost their blooms, but the green shade they provide limits the heat this early in the morning. Brett turns onto Fifty-Fifth Avenue and stands up on the pedals as she starts to climb the hill. She passes by the large brick- column sign that lets everyone in Camden, Tennessee, know that they are now on the campus of Montlake College.

Montlake College is a scene of beauty that the rest of Camden should strive to be like. The beautiful brick buildings, with perfect green lawns, invite students to sit out in the grass and read or study, and there are plenty of students doing just that. Brett pedals faster up through the tree-lined streets. She glides by Griffin Hall, which is the largest building on campus.

Brett is out of breath as she turns right at the back of Griffin Hall. She heads down a quieter section of campus toward a single-story building that looks out of place on such a grand campus. She stops the bike in front of the building. It has glass doors in the front, unlike the other buildings that have large oak doors. Bruschi Hall is the building where the Geology and Paleontology Departments have their classes and offices. It is also a place she knows very well. She has spent large portions of her life exploring the hall, the laboratories, and the offices within it.

Brett looks inside and can't tell if there is anyone there. It is the last summer session, and most of the time the Geology Department has very few students on campus. She opens the door and walks inside. The coolness of the air slams into her, instantly sending a shiver through her body.

She walks into the front office just as she has done hundreds of times. Bruschi Hall is the building where she has spent time with her father before his lectures. She has her corner in his office, and sometimes she would venture into his classes and listen to his lectures on sedimentation or mineralogy. She has always found those subjects fascinating.

Today she is here to continue her research. She has spent hours in the library on campus and at home researching on the computer. It is time to get some questions answered by people that she knows.

The receptionist, a shaggy-haired blond guy in his late twenties, looks up at her when she enters. He smiles. "Hey, good to see you."

Brett smiles back. "How's it goin, Gil?" she replies.

"Ready for senior year."

"So, you're getting outta here?"

"Finally," he says. "It only took seven years."

"Good for you."

"Thank you," he replies.

It looks like he wants to say something else. Brett can sense that it has something to do with her father. Before Gil can start, she says, "I need to see Dr. Brown. Is she here?"

Gil looks down at a sheet of paper on the desk. "She has a class right now."

Brett looks down the hallway toward the classrooms. She motions toward a doorway down the hall. "Do you mind if I wait for her outside her office?"

Gil looks down at the paper again and looks at the office behind his. "Yeah, go ahead," he says.

Brett smiles. "Thank you," she says. She turns and walks down the hallway.

Brett walks by room 106, and she can hear the voice of Dr. Brown, who is talking about igneous rocks and the crystallization of minerals from magma. Brett thinks about stepping inside as she peers into the room. She sees that it is full of students; some of them are attentive to what Dr. Brown is saying, but two students on the back row are sleeping through her speech. A class capacity for the Geology Department at Montlake is ten students, and the lecture hall has precisely ten students. Brett would like to hear Dr. Brown , but she does not want to interrupt her .

Brett walks down the hallway until she comes to an oak-paneled door. The door is rustic, with the stain faded in almost every part. There is a bronze nameplate beside the door that tells everyone that this is the office of Dr. Emily Brown. There is a black folding chair beside the door. Brett takes a seat and waits for the lecture down the hall to end.

Brett is sitting with her head leaning against the wall when she hears talking coming from the receptionist area. She hears the excited voice of Gil down the hallway. The man talking to Gil sounds angry, and he barks an order at him and starts walking down the corridor toward her. She isn't happy with who is walking toward her.

Dr. Sims seems indifferent to everything around him as he walks quickly down the hallway. As he nears the office, he looks at Brett with a surprised look on his face. "Oh, dear," he says with a sneer. "I thought I had seen the last of you when we finished our little investigation."

Brett can't muster any words of response.

He smiles at her, but it is a mocking smile. "I never understood why you were always here, but fortunately for this university and me, we will no longer be subjected to your presence."

Brett grits her teeth. The rage is starting to flow in her body. Down from the deepest part of her soul, the anger of losing her father is ready to erupt out of her like lava from a volcano. "My dad never liked you, Dr. Sims," she says boldly. "And to tell you the truth, what he always said about you is true."

Dr. Sims leans down. His face is inches from hers. "And what did your daddy say?"

"He said you were a pompous windbag—who paid for a degree."

"Is that so?" he responds.

"Those are the things that I can repeat," she says.

Dr. Sims stands up and looks down the hallway. The class from room 106 has ended, and the students are filing out and walking toward the entrance. Dr. Sims turns, and his smile is evil. "Your daddy was a fool for conducting unwarranted experiments." He smiles. "As you know, our investigation, along with that of the police department, proves that his machine was highly unstable and led to his death."

"You know that's not true!" she screams.

"Ah, but it is," he jeers. "Your dear old daddy killed himself and another professor because he was reckless."

Brett is shaking with fury as Dr. Brown walks down the hall toward them. Brett is ready to explode, but before she can give a snarky response, Dr. Brown's voice booms in the hallway. "Dr. Sims!" she says. "What is the meaning of this?"

Dr. Sims turns and smiles at her. "Dr. Brown. I was informing our guest here that her visits will no longer be needed."

Dr. Brown glares at him.

"You see, the recklessness of her father is sure to manifest itself in her. I do have a duty to protect this department and its integrity."

Brett looks away from Dr. Sims. She has a strong desire to punch and kick any part of him that she can get to, but that would prove that "recklessness" is prevalent in her. She looks away, biting the inside of her mouth.

Dr. Brown looks down at her. "She is my guest and is welcome whenever I am here."

Dr. Sims laughs. "We shall see about that," he replies as he turns and walks down the hallway.

Dr. Brown looks over at Brett and shrugs. "He is just a bit unbalanced after our expedition."

Brett glares with penetrating eyes as Sims walks away. "Thank you for that, Dr. Brown," she replies.

Dr. Brown opens the door to the office, and she motions for Brett to step inside.

The office is small and a little stuffy. There is a metal desk that sits in the center of the room with a metal bookcase behind it. The cabinet is filled with rock samples and books about igneous rocks. Dr. Brown is an expert in rocks, h ow they are formed, w hat they are made of. Brett has always found it fascinating how and why rocks are created. Brett sits in the metal folding chair and looks across at Dr. Brown.

"What can I do for you?" Dr. Brown asks.

"I need to ask you a few questions."

"Still working on the disappearance?"

"They're alive!" Brett responds. "I'm going to figure it out."

"I will help you in any way that I can, but the likelihood of them being alive is slim."

"I'm doing this, Dr. Brown."

Dr. Brown leans back in her chair and motions for Brett to ask her questions.

Brett rubs her hands together. "I need you to help me understand how magnetic anomalies form and how their amplification can change the existing structure of space around them."

Dr. Brown runs her hands through her hair. She appears to be formulating a question instead of an answer. Brett leans closer, anticipating that she is ready to speak.

"Magnetic anomalies and changing the structure of space?"

"I know what I saw, Professor," Brett replies. "That is the only thing that makes sense."

"We didn't *see* anything. We searched that canyon—there was nothing."

"I know, but what if the anomaly stopped when that humming sound stopped?"

"That is impossible," Dr. Brown replies.

There is a knock at the door. Dr. Brown looks up. "Yes?"

Gil opens the door and looks inside. "This is odd," he says. "We just received a delivery." Gil looks at Brett, and he is holding a package that is wrapped in brown paper and tied with a string.

"How is that odd?" Dr. Brown asks.

Gil stares at Brett and points. "It' s for her."

CHAPTER 3

Searching for Answers

Gil walks in and gives the bundled package to Brett.

"Thanks," she says, stunned.

Gil turns and leaves the room, closing the door quietly behind him. Brett looks from the package to Dr. Brown, who has a questioning expression on her face. Seeing that she is asking a question without actually *asking* it, Brett shrugs.

Dr. Brown leans across the desk. "Who?"

"Who would know that I would be here?" Brett exclaims.

Dr. Brown shakes her head, trying to see the name on the return address. That part of the package is blank. "This is truly curious," Dr. Brown says as she sits back in her chair.

She looks up at the ceiling, and Brett can see that her mind is working frantically. Dr. Brown is trying to figure out how this package arrived and who sent it. Brett is thinking the same way as she runs her hands across the brittle brown paper.

"I guess I should open it, " she says. "That would solve the 'What is it?' mystery." Brett takes the string in her hand that binds the paper to the package and begins untying it. She lets the rope fall to the floor and sits, waiting to pull the wrinkled wrapper from the package. She looks up at Dr. Brown, who appears nervous but also a little excited. Brett bites her lip and pulls the paper off, and it falls to the floor. She is holding her father's diary—the very diary he had let her examine the night before he disappeared.

Brett stares intently at the book and turns it over in her hands. The cracked, worn leather cover is rough to the touch, and she can feel the scratches and indentations in it . How did it get here? There is nothing that remains of her father and Dr. Mies. All their gear is missing, including the magnetoscope—and, up until now, this book.

She turns the book over and opens the cover. She can see her father's messy handwriting on the first page: "The answers lie in a riddle, and the riddle clarifies what has been hidden. In deciphering t he riddle, we will truly understand the complexities of earth." These words are scrawled on the very first page of the field book. Brett glances up at Dr. Brown.

Dr. Brown is studying her with a furrowed brow. "What is it?" she asks.

Brett is not quite sure how to answer. She is experiencing a bit of shock holding the field book, and her mind races as she tries to figure out who sent it to her. She also wonders how they kno w that she would be here. Without her father working at the college, why would Brett be here? All these thoughts rush over her and nearly overwhelm her.

She stares absently at the first line in the book: "The answers lie in a riddle." What does that mean? Was her dad trying to relay information that only she would understand? Brett closes her eyes and tries to focus her mind on the problem. She takes a few deep breaths and opens her eyes.

Dr. Brown has a concerned look on her face. "Is something wrong, Brett?" she asks.

Brett doesn't know how much she can truly trust Dr. Brown. Rock kept the book a secret for a reason. Was she going to compromise her dad's secret by sharing it with Dr. Brown? She could surely trust her best friends mother with this information.

Brett needed a minute to think by herself. "Dr. Brown, if you would excuse me, I need to . . .u h. . go for a second." Brett stands up, holding the book tightly in her hands. "I'll be back in a few minutes."

Dr. Brown stands up with her arms outstretched, but Brett has already opened the door and hurried from the office. Dr. Brown stares after her in disbelief, thinking, *What is going on?*

Brett rushes down the hallway. Her mind races. She wonders who sent her her father's journal. She also can't figure out the words that are scribbled on the first page. What do they mean? She opens the door and hurries into the bathroom. She is breathing heavily, and she has a death grip on the book. She looks into the mirror. She looks exhausted. Her face is pale, and her hair is disheveled, falling in all directions over her head.

What do I do? she asks herself.

She turns from her reflection, not happy with her reflection's response. Should she confide in Dr. Brown? Should she tell her that this is the field book her dad carried the day he disappeared? Dr. Brown would have a million questions about what is in the book.

Brett closes her eyes and takes a few deep breaths to calm herself. The words her dad has taught her come quickly to her mind: "Observation and analysis are vital to scientific discovery." What has she observed? A man has disappeared, and this book could be the key to finding him. She begins thinking quickly, with different hypotheses flowing into her mind as fast as she asks a question.

"I need a chance to investigate the book," she says. "I need to find out more about how Dad found the place in New Mexico."

She paces the floor in the bathroom, talking loudly to herself. Luckily for her, there isn't another person in the bathroom with her. If someone came in, they would surely think she has lost her mind. "I need to know how he knew the city would appear on July ninth ," she says. "I need to know everything." She paces faster. She puts her hands to her head, massaging her scalp. "I'm going to need help."

After ten minutes, Brett returns to Dr. Brown's office. Dr. Brown offers her a seat, but Brett shakes her head. She holds the book up, so Dr. Brown can see it. "This is my dad's journal," Brett says. "He had this with him when he went missing. I don't know how it ended up here, but I think I can use it to find him."

Dr. Brown crosses her arms, pondering this new information. "He's gone," Dr. Brown says.

Brett shakes the book in her hand violently. "He never went anywhere without his journal. Never. He sent this to me somehow so that I could get him back. That is what I'm going to do, Dr. Brown. I'm bringing him home, but I'm going to need some help."

Her words echo around the office, and Dr. Brown is impressed with the determination of someone so young. Dr. Brown smiles at Brett's devotion to her father. "I will help you, Brett. We will find him."

The door creaks behind Brett. She narrows her eyes. Could someone have been listening from the hallway? Surely not. She walks over and closes the door, then turns, her eyes narrowed for the next task. "I came over here today to ask about electromagnetic anomalies and how they could impact the surrounding environment," she says.

Dr. Brown looks at her, surprised.

"Now I'm going to need a whole lot more information if I'm going to solve this," Brett says in a matter-of-fact tone.

Dr. Brown looks at her door. "All right," she says. "I would like for you to come over to the house this evening. Natalie will be there, and she can help."

Brett nods and holds the book tightly in her hands. "Tonight, it is," she replies. "We're going to find them."

Brett leaves the building and hops on her bike. She is energized by the prospect of finding her dad and also solving a mystery in the process. She pedals down Fifty-fif th Avenue, gliding under the trees that line the roadway. It is almost noon, and the traffic on the street has picked up a little. There are more cars on the road, and she steers carefully through the lines of automobiles. She turns her head, looking behind her. She is readying herself to move her bike over to the sidewalk. As she passes the intersection of Fifty-fifth and Waveland, she notices a black sedan parked along the street. Brett can clearly see the man in the driver's seat. He is wearing a tie and jacket, and he watches her as she speeds by his sedan.

Brett steers her bike onto the sidewalk and pedals harder. She looks back. T he black sedan has pulled onto Fifty-fif th and is driving at a pace that will not pass her. Her heart beats faster and faster. Maybe she is only paranoid. She looks around as she rides on the sidewalk, trying to find an intersecting street that she can speed down. If the black-sedan guy is following her, then the alteration of her route will prove it.

She stops pedaling fast and instead goes at a casual speed. She acts as if nothing is out of the ordinary. She can see the next intersection up ahead, and as she nears it, she decides to make the turn rather quickly. She makes a sharp right and casually looks over her shoulder at the black sedan. The driver looks at her as she turns, but he continues going straight on Fifty-fif th Avenue.

Brett breathes a sigh of relief and picks up the speed, hurrying to-ward home. At the rate she is going, she might not make it by twelve. Brett does not want to explain to Grandpa Jake the reason for arriving home so late. He wouldn't believe her if she told him that a man in a black sedan was chasing her through Camden.

Brett stands up on the pedals and races through the campus down onto the main road. She speeds across traffic, and cars honk as she steers around them. Finally, she pulls into the gravel driveway of the farm. The gravel crunches under the tires as she nears the house. She looks down at her watch. One minute past twelve—she almost made it.

She leans the bike against the cellar door and starts to run around the house. The black sedan drives along the main road, going much more slowly than the recommended speed limit. She can see the driver looking up at the house.

Brett races around the house, her hair flying out behind her as she runs. She gets up the steps in a flash and hurries inside, locking the door quickly behind her. She walks through the living room, looking through each window as she passes them. She can see the black car slowly driv-ing down the road, with the driver still looking up at the house.

"Not good," she says. She steps away from the window and begins pacing around the floor. "They know," she says. "Whoever it is, they know I have it."

"What do you have?" Grandpa Jake says.

Brett jumps in the air. She turns with her hand on her chest. Her eyes are wide, and she has a look of extreme fear on her face. "Oh, G-G-Grandpa," she stammers.

He motions for her to come into the kitchen. "Come on now," he says. "I have your lunch ready."

She follows Grandpa Jake into the kitchen. She sits down and starts eating the sandwich that he has prepared.

Grandpa Jake sits down across from her and stares at her intently. He drums his fingers on the table as he watches her eat. Brett is aloof. She isn't going to give anything away.

"So how was Natalie?" he asks.

Brett looks up as she chews her food. She swallows and says meekly, "She's fine."

Grandpa Jake eyes her suspiciously, but he finally seems satisfied and stands up. "Can I get you anything else?"

Brett looks up. "No, thank you." She quickly takes another bite and returns her gaze to the sandwich.

Grandpa Jake walks out of the room, leaving Brett alone in the kitchen to ponder a few questions. *Who is the man in the black sedan, and why is he following her?* She is pretty sure it has something to do with the book and her father's disappearance, but why? She finishes her sandwich and walks over to the window. She looks up and down the street. The black sedan isn't parked anywhere on the road. She knows that that man is out there somewhere, and she is sure that when she goes to Natalie's house tonight, the man will be following.

CHAPTER 4

Meeting of the Minds

Brett takes care of the goats in record time. She has them milked, fed, and put up in their stalls. She closes the barn door and walks up toward the house, then looks over her shoulder, checking to see if someone is following her. The creaking office door at Montlake College and the black sedan have put her on edge. Her head swivels from right to left as she gazes, looking for anyone who might be watching.

She opens the gate, her eyes continually searching around her. She closes it quickly and runs up to the house. She needs to get in there to get the book and start her journey over to Dr. Brown's place. What will Dr. Brown say when Brett tells her that someone is following her? Will she believe her? Or will Dr. Brown say Brett is making things up? Brett isn't sure that the professor believes her account of seeing the city of Cibola, but at the moment Dr. Brown is her only ally.

Brett rushes up the steps of the porch, looking out at the road and expecting to see the black sedan stealthily rolling up the street. But t here isn't any sign of the vehicle. Maybe whoever is following her is using more than one. Surely there is more than one person with interest in the book. Brett hurries inside, and the door closes behind her. She races up the steps to her bedroom.

The room is neat and orderly. It is what you would expect from an eleven-year-old girl who is meticulous in everything she does. There are history, science, and sports books on the shelf. Brett enjoys read-ing, and most of the books in her room once belonged to her father. She hurries over to the bed and picks up her blue backpack. Her hands clasp the smooth fabric, and she quickly walks over to the desk. She grabs two spiral-bound notebooks from her desk and places them in her bag. Brett opens the drawer and pulls out the field book, then wraps the book in a linen towel that is on the desk. She zips the bag closed and throws it over her shoulder.

Brett peers out the window, searching for the man who has followed her earlier that day. There is nobody there. It's time to get moving. Brett leaves her tidy room and walks down the stairs. She makes it to the door before she hears the heavy footsteps of Grandpa Jake. She has the doorknob in her hand when he speaks.

"Going out again?" he asks.

"Yes, sir," she says. "Natalie asked me to come over."

"It's good that you are spending time with your friends."

"As you said, I need to get out of the house."

"No need staying in the house," he replies. "I'm not much company for an eleven-year-old girl."

Though she likes spending time with her grandpa, she doesn't like watching the old game shows or home improvement episodes . She smiles at him. "I will be home later."

Grandpa Jake stares at her. She can tell that he wants to know how she will be getting home. He always worries when she rides her bike at night. "Dr. Brown said that they will bring me home."

Grandpa Jake nods his head. "That's good," he says. "I'll see you tonight."

Brett steps out into the late afternoon heat, and the door starts clos-ing behind her. Grandpa Jake yells at her from the living room, "Before you go, I just want to tell you that a gentleman from the life insurance company came by about the distribution from your father's policy."

Brett turns around. "What?"

Grandpa Jake walks over and pulls open the door. "The insurance guy said that the company is ready to release the proceeds of the life insurance policy."

Brett stares at her grandpa in disbelief. She ha dn't thought that there was a policy. Her mind races as she tries to make sense of this new information. "What did the insurance man look like?"

Grandpa Jake leans out the front door. "Skinny guy, brown hair. I don't know. He looked like an insurance guy," he says. "The car he drove wasn't like an insurance guy's, though. A shiny black four-door. Looked like a government car."

Brett turns her head, staring out at the roadway. They have been here. They probably are seeing how easy it is going to be to take the book. That isn't good. Not only is she in danger, but her grandpa is also in danger. She smiles at her grandpa. "That's good news," she says. "That will help, won't it? "

Grandpa Jake nods. "Indeed, it will," he responds. "Well, get going. You don't want to keep Natalie waiting, and thank Dr. Brown for all that she has done for us."

Brett grimaces, "I will."

Brett wraps her arms around Grandpa Jake, squeezing him tightly, then runs down the steps and disappears around the house. Grandpa Jake smiles and walks back into the house.

Brett's mind races all the way over to Natalie's house. Whoever is following her is covering all their bases. She is sure that they are after the book, and she is confident that if they have the book, they will have the keys to Cibola. That is incentive enough for them to take the book from her. She decides that she must keep it safe and solve the mystery that her father has solved.

Dr. Brown lets her in when she knocks on the door. Brett hurries inside, looking over her shoulder. Dr. Brown looks at her questioningly. "What is going on?"

Brett, satisfied that the black sedan isn't outside watching every move she makes, walks over and sits on the couch. "A man has been following me, and I'm sure it has something to do with Dad's field book."

Dr. Brown looks out the panes on the door and locks the door. "Are you sure?" she asks.

Brett nods. "The guy even came by the house and told Grandpa Jake he is looking to release the funds from the life insurance policy that Dad owned." Brett rubs her hands on her cargo pants. She is still wearing her backpack, and she is tapping her leg nervously.

"Oh, dear," Dr. Brown says.

Brett can tell that she is nervous. She looks across the room as Natalie enters. Brett can see the concern on her face. Brett doesn't want to put her best friend and her mother in danger. She looks up at Dr. Brown. "I won't stay long. I need you to help me figure a few things out, and then I will be out of your hair," Brett says stoically.

Natalie looks at her mom as Brett finishes speaking. Natalie is much different than her best friend. Brett is logical and has the mind of a scientist, but Natalie is artsy. She likes to write poetry and songs. Natalie doesn't like science, math, or history. Those are her worst subjects in school, but when Brett came home from New Mexico and Natalie asked her for help, Brett did just that. Natalie has lost track of the books on magnetism that she has read, and though it has been confusing and she has had no idea what the authors were talking about, she has continued.

Natalie pulls at her short brown hair. She looks from her mom to Brett. "What is she talking about?" she says .

Dr. Brown again walks over to the window and peers outside. She looks for a few seconds. Satisfied that no one is watching the house, Dr. Brown closes the curtains and walks over toward the couch.

Natalie stares at her. "What's going on?" she yells. "Why are you looking out the windows, and why is Brett saying she won't stay long?"

"I think there are some bad people after me, and I don't want you two to get hurt."

"Come on," Natalie says, looking at her mother.

"It's true," Brett responds. "They followed me after I left your mom's office."

"Why would they do that?"

Brett unzips her backpack and takes out the field book. She gives it to Natalie. Natalie looks down at the book and then at Brett.

"That is my dad's. He used it to locate the lost city, and I believe that the people who are following me are looking for this."

Natalie looks at Dr. Brown. The scientist stares at her daughter as the color leaves her face. Natalie's eyes are wide, and she is pulling at the sleeve of her mom's shirt. "We're not going to let her go off by herself, are we?" Natalie asks.

Dr. Brown shakes her head no.

"REALLY?!" Natalie yells. "We *are* helping."

"It's all right." Brett says.

"You're not doing this on your own," Natalie responds.

"Look, I don't know what we should do," Dr. Brown says. "This is all so crazy."

Natalie holds the tattered book up in the air and waves it around. "They aren't getting this," she says, before handing it back to Brett. "And we are helping Brett figure out where Dr. Wilson went."

Brett smiles, as her best friend has decided she will not leave her. She will be there to the end. Brett honestly hasn't wanted to do this alone, and now if Natalie agrees, then Dr. Brown will probably go along with it.

"Okay," Dr. Brown says. "Let's try to figure out where Dr. Wilson is, and then we can decide what to do."

"That's not good enough, Mom," Natalie demands.

"Natalie, I will not let anything happen to Brett, all right?"

"Dr. Brown," Brett says, "I—"

"Brett, we are going to help you do whatever it is you need to do," Dr. Brown says.

"I didn't do all of that reading for nothing," Natalie says. "We will find him. Now, what is in that book?"

Dr. Brown sits in the chair and leans over the table as Brett places the book before them and opens it to the third page. There is a map of the southwestern part of the United States. There are three red lines on the map, showing three routes. The handwriting there is hard to decipher. It looks like her dad wrote the notes quickly. His writing has never been neat, and when he was in a hurry, it became almost unreadable.

Brett traces her figure across the letters as she says, " E-S-T-E-B-A-N. " Brett looks up at Dr. Brown. "Ever heard of Esteban?"

Dr. Brown shakes her head. "Never."

Brett looks over at Natalie, who smiles. "You know *I* haven't."

The next line on the map has the name Friar Marcos de Niza under it. That name doesn't ring any bells either. The final sentence has the name Coronado. Francisco Coronado, she knows . Her dad has told her many stories when she was young about Coronado. He has recited stories about conquistadors, just like other dads tell their daughters stories about princesses.

Brett turns the faded yellow page. The next page, she says, begins, " 'I, Estebanico, this day, May 30, 1535, have seen the golden parapets of a faraway city. A city that many of the peoples in this land have mentioned with awe and reverence. A city of wealth unimaginable.' "

It is the diary of Esteban, transcribed in the legible handwriting of Dr. Wilson. He has taken great care to write every letter legibly. On the opposite of each page of the diary is the original text, written in Spanish. "My goodness," Dr. Brown says. "This is extraordinary. It looks like these are the actual pages from a real diary."

Brett runs her fingers down the creased and weathered page and continues reading the diarist's words. " 'I, Estebanico, on this day, July 31, 1535, have finally found the entrance to the vast city. The people who populate the city were quite hospitable and treated me with dignity and respect. It is in direct contrast to how the Spaniards treat people they view as uneducated heathens. These men and women have a vast knowledge of science, art, and philosophy. (They remind me of Sa' adi, the rulers of my own country.) We talked about the riches of their city, how they came to possess so much gold that they wrapped their building in it. They told me that the metal flowed from the ground. This is interesting, I think.'"

Brett turns the page. She is engrossed in the words of the man named Esteban. It reads like a novel. His words are very descriptive, and she

wants to finish the diary. After all, this is about the place where her father has disappeared. Brett looks up and sees that Dr. Brown and Natalie are just as interested as she is in the outcome of Esteban's story. Brett
can see that Dr. Brown is formulating some hypothesis in her mind as
the diary is being read.

Brett continues until they reach the end of the diary. "' I have lost
my way and can no longer see the city. The gold-and-turquoise em-
blems are no more. Why am I forsaken? I have lost paradise, and I cannot find my way back inside.' "

Brett stares at the last line. " 'I have lost paradise.' " She looks up at
Natalie. "What do you think that means?" Brett asks.

"I guess you can go in and come out," Natalie replies.

"Dr. Wilson was searching for electromagnetic anomalies, " Dr.
Brown says.

"Mom, you're talking to a kid."

"The earth generates electromagnetic fields because of the core and
spin . Now, there is some variableness to the spin, and . . ."

"Kid, " Natalie interjects.

"The electromagnetism changes. It can act as a cover for something.
One minute it' s there, and the next it' s gone."

"So you're saying the city is like a magician. Disappearing and reap-
pearing whenever it wants," Natalie says.

Brett looks over at her. Her mind races over thoughts of magnetic
fields acting like a light being turned on and off. *What happens when
the light goes out? How do you turn it back on?* Her dad has known the
answer, and it is here in the diary.

"If Esteban went into the city and came out of it, and he could not
locate it after he left, that could correspond to what Dr. Wilson was
studying," Dr. Brown sa ys.

"Electromagnetism," Brett says with her eyes wide. "That could hide
the city, and the only way to find it is by locating the strong magnetic
field."

"What we are working on at Montlake is how to identify electromagnetic anomalies and then understand what those anomalies do to the environment," Dr. Brown says.

"You think these electromagnetic anomalies can impact the air around them?" Brett asks.

"It is possible," Dr. Brown responds, staring off in the distance.

"Could you disappear?" Natalie asks .

Dr. Brown looks down at her with a "you- didn't- just- ask- that-question" expression on her face.

"Dr. Wilson disappeared into thin air," Natalie responds. "What if this anomaly causes thin air, and you pass right through it like a doorway, without even knowing it? Like the Bermuda Triangle."

Dr. Brown is staring into space, drumming her fingers on her chin.

Natalie looks away from her mother and stares at Brett. "What do you think about that? Could it be possible?"

Brett is turning the brown, brittle pages of the book. She reads the account of the Franciscan monk Marcos de Niza, who said that he saw the city but did not go in. How did this monk get a glimpse of the city? Finally, she reads the account of Coronado. At the very end of the diary, her dad ha s written the words *Coronado's door*. The words are underlined with three thick black lines. Brett looks over at Natalie. "What did you say about a door?"

Natalie looks at her, happy that someone is finally listening to what she has to say. "What if the electromagnetism causes the air to become thin, and when you enter the thin air, it acts as a doorway to somewhere else?"

Brett points down to the words. Natalie looks down and sees *Coronado's door*. Natalie's mouth falls open, and her eyes get as wide as a pair of binocular lenses. Brett looks from the book to Natalie. They can hear Dr. Brown say, "Coronado's door? Could happen."

"A door could open?" Natalie asks.

Dr. Brown looks at her with a vacant expression. "We have been producing strong electromagnetic disturbances in the lab. They are localized, but they did create a small void."

Brett looks up from the book. "That is how Esteban went to the city. My dad is there now."

Dr. Brown blinks and looks at her. "It is possible," Dr. Brown says. "But I don't know how to find it again. We see from reading the diary that it took Esteban four years to get back to the city."

Brett closes her eyes. The idea of her dad spending four years in Cibola causes a lump to form in her throat. She closes the field book and holds it close to her chest. "There has to be a way into the city that won't require us to wait that long," Brett says as she grips the book tighter.

CHAPTER 5

The Great Escape

Brett and Natalie continue looking through the field book, making notes in the pages of the notebook. They look at the map that shows Coronado's pathway through the southwest. "It's hard to believe that he never found the city," Natalie says.

Brett glances up at her. "What if he found it?" she replies. "He did split his expedition into smaller groups, and there were times that he was absent from the others."

"I guess it's possible," Natalie says.

"I bet he found the doorway too. Just like Esteban," Brett replies.

"We just need to follow in the footstep of Coronado," Natalie says matter-of-factly.

"Follow Coronado and find my dad."

"Exactly," Natalie says. "We have come a long way in the last few hours, and I'm sure that we will find him."

Brett jumps off the couch and looks at her watch. It is nearly ten o'clock. "Oh no!" she exclaims. "Grandpa Jake is going to be so upset that I'm getting home so late. Can I borrow your phone?"

"Of course, " Dr. Brown replies.

Brett walks to the kitchen and picks up the phone. She punches the numbers on the hand set. She taps her foot nervously as the phone dials. It then rings once, twice, three times. The phone continues ringing. This is not good. Grandpa Jake wouldn't let the phone ring that many times. He hates phones, and he has always threatened to get rid of it. "He's not answering ," she says. "Something's wrong."

"Maybe we should call the police, " Dr. Brown suggests .

"Not yet, " Brett says sternly.

"It's okay," Natalie responds. "We' ll take you home, and if there' s someone there, we will get them."

"Get your bag and the notes that we have made," Dr. Brown says.

Brett picks up her bag and places the field book and the notes inside. She zips the bag closed, making sure it is secure. She slings the bag over her shoulder and walks toward the door. Dr. Brown grabs her keys from the table beside the front door, and Natalie opens the door. Natalie walks out onto the lit porch first, and the light transmits a robust yellow glow out into the darkness of the neighborhood.

Brett steps out onto the porch behind Natalie. Her senses are alert with the prospect of meeting the people who want the journal. She can hear the rumble of tires on the road a few streets over. The fear of what is lurking at the end of the yellow light sends a shiver up her spine, and the thought that those faceless individuals are out there waiting makes her skin tingle. She strains her ears, listening for the slightest out-of-the-ordinary sound. Dr. Brown hurries by the two girls and races over to the blue Ford Escape parked in the driveway. Brett and Natalie hurry behind her.

A car engine roars to life up the street from where they are standing. "Get in!" Brett yells.

Dr. Brown throws open the door and jumps into the driver's seat. Natalie opens the door and hops inside. Brett looks up the dark street. A light instantly flashes, and the black sedan begins moving quickly toward the driveway.

The driveway at the house is very narrow. It can accommodate one car, and in front of the Ford is the garage. The only way out is backward onto the street. The black sedan races toward the driveway. "We need to move," Natalie says.

Dr. Brown slams the SUV into reverse and hits the gas . The tires squeal as she careens backward toward the street. The front of the black sedan streaks in front of the driveway just as the Ford Escape erupts out into the street.

Dr. Brown drives down the dark street in reverse, steering wildly from one side of the road to the other. Brett points toward the house. "He's turning around."

Dr. Brown narrows her eyes and presses her foot down on the accelerator. The car whines and speeds faster down the dark avenue. As they near the intersection, Dr. Brown grits her teeth. "I've never done anything like this, so hold on." She slams her foot on the brake and turns the wheel to the left. The car veers quickly up the side street, and before it comes to a stop, Dr. Brown slams the car into drive and races away from the intersection.

She looks through the rearview mirror and scans the side mirrors. "Do you see them back there?" she asks.

Brett stares intently out into the darkness. Suddenly headlights appear down the street behind them. "Here they come," Brett says. She doesn't take her eyes off the sedan following them. Her heart races as the bright lights grow larger and larger behind them as they race in the darkness. It seems like these people are serious about getting their hands on the journal. If they get the book, then they will have a direct line to the first city of gold. She is sure that these people will stop at nothing to find all those riches.

Brett looks over at Natalie. Natalie stares out the window and then back at her mom. "They're gaining on us," Natalie says. "You need to lose them."

Dr. Brown looks up into the mirror and then out at the road. Brett can see her through the mirror. She is focused on steering and continuously on the lookout for a way to escape the car pursuing them.

The two cars speed along Cherry Street, which has trees that hang over the roadway. The trunks flash by in a blur as they race west. "How are we going to lose them?" Natalie asks frantically .

Dr. Brown turns sharply to the right onto Walnut Street. The tires squeal loudly, and Dr. Brown presses the pedal to the floor. The Escape whines and speeds off to the north. Brett watches as the sedan turns effortlessly onto the street. The driver of the pursuing car looks as though they have been in a high-speed chase before.

Natalie leans up on the front seat. "Take that street," she says, pointing ahead.

Dr. Brown looks over at her.

"Don't worry. We can make a few quick turns in here and lose this guy," Natalie says confidently.

Dr. Brown turns the Escape down Bent Oak Ave. The curves on the road look like the curved branches of an oak tree. Brett still has her eyes fixed on the intersection behind her. "He hasn't made the turn yet."

Dr. Brown nods and turns the lights off quickly.

The car is traveling at a high rate of speed down the empty and dark roadway. One small mistake, and their escape will be over. Natalie points. "Turn now," she says a little too loudly.

Dr. Brown steers down another dark street and races onward. "How's it look back there, Brett?" she asks .

"He isn't behind us," Brett responds.

"Take a right up here," Natalie says, like she is leading the getaway.

Dr. Brown turns, and after a few more turns without the black sedan following, she slows down to the recommended speed limit of forty-five miles per hour. "Well, this couldn't get any worse," Dr. Brown says. Her hands are shaking, and she tries to hide it by gripping the steering wheel tighter. She turns the lights on, and the headlights cut through the darkness.

Brett holds her bag tightly and continues looking behind her.

"They could have caught us," Natalie replies.

"We need a place to go so we can figure out what to do," Dr. Brown says.

"I need to check on Grandpa Jake!" Brett exclaims. "I hope they haven't done anything to him."

"That might be a little dangerous at the moment," Dr. Brown states. "If they have been watching our house, you can bet they are watching yours. I think we should call the police. This is getting really serious."

"The police won't do anything. There isn't anyone chasing us anymore."

"Yeah, M om. Two kids and one crazy mom talking about men in black chasing them through town. They will believe that."

"All right, " Dr. Brown says. "We are smart. Let's think."

Brett says, "I can't leave him there."

"You may have to," Dr. Brown responds.

"I won't!" Brett shouts.

"Mom, it's her grandfather. You can't expect her to leave him behind," Natalie says.

Dr. Brown drums her hands on the steering wheel. Her eyes dart from the road to the rearview mirror. She isn't comfortable with being chased all over town. "Okay," she says. "We're going to swing by my office and pick up a few things. Then we will go by and get Grandpa Jake," Dr. Brown states. Her eyes meet Brett's in the mirror, and Brett nods her approval. "When we get to the office, we get in and get out. Got me?"

Both girls nod. Dr. Brown narrows her eyes and drives the speed limit all the way to Montlake College.

CHAPTER 6

Finding Anomalies

D r. Brown drives the Ford Escape around the rear entrance of Bruschi Hall. She leaves the car running and waits. "Girls, keep your eyes open."

Both girls reply, "Right."

They sit in the Escape, watching all around them. After five minutes , Dr. Brown finally turns to Brett and Natalie. "Time to go in," she says. "Stick close to me."

Brett and Natalie look at each other and nod. "Let's go," Natalie says.

They open the doors and stare out into the shadows of the parking lot. It is almost ten-thirty in the evening, and the campus is eerily quiet. Brett strains her ears, trying to hear the faintest sound of someone waiting for them in the shadows. She hears her breathing in her ears, and her heart is beating so fast she can feel it in her ears as well. With her senses tuned into the surroundings, the three run over to the door. Dr. Brown has her keys out before they reach the entrance. She slips the key into the lock quickly and turns the handle. The lock clicks, and Dr. Brown opens the door and ushers the girls into the back entrance of Bruschi Hall.

The hallway is empty as they step into the building. Bruschi Hall is usually vacant at this time of night, even during the fall and spring semesters. The building's safety lights are on in the hallway, casting a strange glow on the walls. Dr. Brown hurries down the hall toward her office, which is five doors down from the rear entrance. Brett and Natalie run behind her.

Dr. Brown still has her keys out when she makes it to her office door. She quickly unlocks the door, and the three hurry inside. Dr. Brown uses the pull chain on the lamp that sits on her desk. A bright-orange glow fills the room. "Natalie, get my field bag out of the cabinet," she says.

Natalie strides across the office and opens the door, then grabs the black canvas bag that is crumpled up on the bottom. She hauls it out, straining to lift it to the height of her knees. It feels like it weighs a hundred pounds. "Man, this is heavy," Natalie says.

Dr. Brown glances up from her desk as she opens the drawers and pulls out three field books, then hands them to Brett. "Hold on to these. We might need them."

Brett grabs them and stuffs them into her bag.

Dr. Brown checks her watch as she finds more of her field notes from the trip to New Mexico. "This data should help us with deciphering what is in your book, Brett."

"All your field notes from the expedition?" Brett asks.

"Every one of them," she replies. "I also kept some of Dr. Mies's notes."

"Really?" Brett sounds surprised.

"Dr. Mies was—*is* a very gifted geophysicist," Dr. Brown says. "The magnetoscope that he was using, that was his design, and if I'm not mistaken, I believe your father gave him the specifications for its construction."

Brett smiles broadly. She always likes hearing about her father's accomplishments. Brett enjoys his success much more than her own. As she thinks about the design and function of the magnetoscope, a thought crashes through her mind. "Do you believe there is another magnetoscope here?"

Dr. Brown stares at her as if she is processing large amounts of information, and it is slowing down her brain.

"They built it here, right?" Brett asks.

"Of course," Dr. Brown replies.

"Does it make sense that they might have made another one, just in case?" Brett asks.

"It's possible," Dr. Brown responds.

"If I were getting ready to find a city of gold, I would make a back-up," Brett says.

Natalie walks over, dragging the black bag across the floor. "I would too."

Dr. Brown stares at the two girls and checks her watch one more time. She looks at the desk again, making sure that she has everything she needs. Satisfied with all the information she has gathered, and happy with the shortness of time it has taken to get all her gear, she grabs the bag from Natalie and hoists it onto her shoulder. "Time to go."

Brett looks up at her. "What about the second magnetoscope?"

"We don't have time," Dr. Brown says a little too forcefully.

"We're going to need it if we ever hope to find my dad!" Brett exclaims.

Dr. Brown walks across the room to the door. She looks back at the two girls, motioning them to move. "All right," she says quickly. "Dr. Sims had both Dr. Mies's and your father's offices cleaned out and the boxes put into the storage room in the mineralogy lab. The magneto-scope should be there—if there is a second one." She slowly opens the door and peers up and down the dark hallway.

The silence in the building is unnerving, and Brett tries to summon her strength to find the magnetoscope.

"Where is the lab?" Natalie asks.

"In the basement," Brett and Dr. Brown say unison.

"Of course it is," Natalie says. "Every time a person in a movie is being chased and they need to get something to help them, it is always in the dark, creepy basement."

Brett is standing behind her, holding her breath. The "dark, creepy basement" comment causes her mind to race. "What if the man from the black sedan is down there?" she asks herself a little too loudly.

Natalie looks at her with her eyes wide. "You think he's already down there?" she says nervously.

Brett shakes her head. "No, I don't. Just thinking out loud." Brett watches Dr. Brown intently.

Dr. Brown motions with her arm that it is time to move. They go out of the office in a single-file line, staying close to the wall. They quietly hurry toward the glowing red sign on the wall that reads *Exit*. Dr. Brown opens the door slowly. The door doesn't make a sound as it swings on its hinges. They listen for any sounds coming from the basement of the building. They stand motionless in the doorway for what seems like five minutes. Satisfied, Dr. Brown leads them down the stairs, and the sound of their feet falling on the concrete steps echoes up the lit stairwell.

They come to a stop at a large wooden door that has a black sign with white letters: *Geology Laboratory*. Dr. Brown grabs the handle.

Brett feels the excitement of finding the magnetoscope, but she also has fear creeping into her mind. Her heart is beating wildly in her chest, and she has sweat beads forming above her brow. Could the man who has been following her be down here, ready to strike her? Brett closes her eyes. She isn't going to let the thought of him possibly being down here take her focus away from her goal. Brett takes a few deep breaths before Dr. Brown finally opens the door.

"Do we need this magneto thing?" Natalie asks.

Brett nods, giving her the signal that yes, this piece of equipment is vital to finding the lost city.

"Just making sure," Natalie says.

Dr. Brown steps out into the carpeted hallway. The basement level appears to be deserted, so they hurry down the hall toward the last rooms on the right. The first room says that it is the petrology lab. The final room has a sign on the door that reads *Mineralogy Lab—Caution*. Dr. Brown takes out her keys again. Her hands are shaking as she inserts the room key into the lock. The door clicks, and they hurry inside.

Once inside, Dr. Brown turns on the lights. The bright fluorescent bulbs ignite and fill the room with cascading white light. "This way,"

Dr. Brown whispers. They move along a series of benches that hold cutting tools and mounting slides for making rock cross-sections. There are two large circular saws on the center table. Natalie stares at them as they walk by, shaking her head. "You knew that there would be large saws in the creepy basement. You just had to know it," she says.

In the back corner is the storage room. All the lab supplies and scientific equipment are kept in the small alcove, which is the size of a closet. The room is perfectly still and quiet. Brett can hear her ragged breath as she stands by the door to the storage room. "It has to be in there," she says.

"I don't want to know what is in there. I've seen enough out here," Natalie says.

"We get in, find it, and get out quickly," Brett says.

"What does this magnetosphere look like?" Natalie asks. "I've never seen one."

"Looks like an iPad, just thicker," Brett responds.

"Got it," Natalie replies.

Dr. Brown opens the door. The temperature inside is much colder than the laboratory, and it causes chill bumps to appear on Brett's arm.

Dr. Brown flips the light switch, and the dull white light of the fluorescent bulbs envelopes the room. "The boxes from Dr. Mies's office should be back here somewhere," Dr. Brown says, walking toward a row of boxes.

Brett rushes over to them and quickly pulls one open. She take s out the contents of the box. There are books about the orientation of sediments in marine environments, lava flows in the Pacific Ocean, and basaltic rocks and their minerals. She places the books back inside and searches the next box.

Dr. Brown and Natalie are searching through the other boxes. After five minutes of look ing, they do not find a second magnetoscope. "Maybe he didn't make another one," Dr. Brown conjectures .

Brett climbs over the boxes stacked in front of her. She remains confident that the device is somewhere in the room. Dr. Brown and Natalie watch as Brett opens another container. "We already looked through that one," Natalie says softly.

There is ringing in Brett's ears. She is starting to panic, and she tears the top off a box to look inside. "It has to be here!" she says, gritting her teeth. "It *has* to be."

Dr. Brown watches her with a grimace on her face. "Brett."

Brett hurries from box to box, throwing their contents on the floor. "I know it's here. He wouldn't have made only one. Dad would have made two." Her eyes are filled with tears as she throws books and papers out of the boxes.

"Brett, we need to get going," Dr. Brown says kindly.

"We can't. We just can't," Brett says. She turns, looking in every direction for a box they haven't searched.

Natalie hurries around the table and puts her arm around Brett. "Come on. It's time to get out of here."

Tears are streaming down Brett's face as she lets Natalie lead her around the boxes. At the end of the row, she sees a box sitting on a table. Brett hasn't looked through that box yet, and she is sure that her friends haven't either. Brett pulls free from Natalie and hurries over to the box, pulling it open.

Her chin falls as she looks inside. There is nothing in the box but a pile of black rocks. The tears leak from her eyes quickly as she stares at the broken basalts. She gasps for breath as the realization of her failure sets in. The magnetoscope isn't here, and now there is no way that she will ever find her dad. What is she going to do now? How will she be able to go on without him? Another thought flashes through her mind: *It doesn't matter if the man in the black sedan gets the book now.* Her quest to find the city has just ended in a box full of rocks.

She looks up a Natalie, who is crying too. "I'm sorry, Brett."

Brett looks back at the black and broken rocks sitting in the bottom of the container. There is a metallic gleam coming from the right side of the box where she has thrown the cover. The fluorescent white light somehow reflects off the metal. Her heart beats rapidly as she grabs the sheet and pulls it away from the table. She gasps as she looks down—the second magnetoscope.

Brett slowly reaches down and picks up the device. She smiles broadly and turns to Natalie and Dr. Wilson. "We have it. Now we can find him!" Brett exclaims . Brett hurries around the final boxes, and the three of them stride toward the door. As they make it to the door, Dr. Sims steps out from the mineralogy lab with a sneer on his pale face.

Trapped

D r. Sims is standing in the middle of the doorway. He shakes his head as he looks from Dr. Brown to Brett, who casually moves the magnetoscope into the right-side pocket of her pants. It is a tight fit, but she hopes that Dr. Sims won't see. The smile on his face is one of those smiles a person gives when they have caught someone doing something wrong. "What brings you here so late at night, Dr. Brown?" he asks with a chuckle. He watches Brett as he waits for Dr. Brown's response.

Brett can hear her heart beating in her chest. The beating is wild, as if her heart is trying to break free from the constraints of her ribcage. She can feel her face flush and the heat swelling in her as the anger crashes haphazardly through her body. She hates Dr. Sims, and with the look in his eyes, she thinks that he could be the one who is having her followed. She does not look away from Dr. Sims. She glares at him with utter disdain.

"I needed to retrieve some data from a field study," Dr. Brown lies.

"Oh, come now, Dr. Brown," he sneers. "You are here for something far more valuable than some boring field data."

"No, Dr. Sims. I assure you that is why I am here."

He laughs boisterously, his whole body shaking as she finishes her statement. He never leaves the doorway. He knows that the door is the only way for them to escape, and he remains firmly planted on the spot.

"You could have gotten that anytime, but here you are in the dead of night, skulking around the dreaded storage closet." His stare remains on Brett, waiting for her to respond to his words. "And why would you bring your daughter and the brat with you? Shouldn't they be in bed at such a late hour?"

Brett grits her teeth and clenches her fists. She wants to fly across the room and knock that sneer off his pale, weaselly face.

He laughs again. "I see that my words have upset you," Dr. Sims says to Brett, his eyes narrowing. I want the book that was delivered today," Dr. Sims snarls. "And I want the location of Cibola."

"Cibola?" Brett questions.

"That is the real reason that we went on our excursion to New Mexico, is it not?"

"I don't—," Brett starts.

"Silly girl," he spits. "Do you think I didn't know what your pathetic father was doing? Do you think I didn't know that he was trying to put himself above this university—and me?"

"You're a terrible person," Brett responds vociferously.

"Rock Wilson is not fit for such a discovery," he continues. "I, on the other hand, *am* fit, and I will make this grand discovery and bring it to the world."

"My dad already discovered it," she responds.

"I'm afraid you are mistaken again," he laughs. "Rock Wilson is dead, gone, never returning."

"You're wrong!" she says vehemently.

"Now, give me the book."

"What are you talking about?" Dr. Brown responds.

"Don't play dumb with me," he jeers. "I know you received a book by courier this afternoon. I know that you took that book home with you, and I am sure that it is here with all of us now."

"You're the one who has been following us!" Brett yells, unable to control her anger.

"Why would I want to follow you?" he snarls. "Just like your father. Stupid and quite unobservant."

"My dad—," Brett starts.

Dr. Sims laughs loudly as he walks into the room. He pushes his chest out and holds his head high in a very dignified, supercilious manner. "Your father was useless to this university," he scoffs. "Unlike the other professors, your dear father never produced one published study. What kind of scientist never publishes any work? A terrible one."

Brett grinds her teeth together, and the pressure causes her jaw to ache. Her fingernails are digging into her palms, and she can feel a searing pain shooting through her hands. She is ready to pounce on him and make him pay for the disparaging words he is saying about her father.

"You haven't been following us?" Dr. Brown asks.

"Just give me the book, and the three of you can leave," Dr. Sims replies.

Dr. Brown takes her phone out of her bag. "I am calling the police."

Dr. Sims laughs, "And you think they will come down here? " He sneers. "You're as foolish as this silly girl." He acts quickly, snatching the phone from her shaking hands. "Now one last time. Give me the book."

Dr. Brown looks over at Brett, trying to get her attention, but Brett is already thinking of a way to get out of the storage room. "If we give it to you, you' ll let us go?" Brett asks shrewdly.

Dr. Sims smiles and uses his right index finger to cross his heart. "You have my word," he jeers.

Brett opens her bag and takes out the field book. She holds it tightly in her hands and observes Dr. Sims with her eyes narrowed. His face becomes more rigid as he sees the book in her hands. He extends his hands, waiting for the book, and the smirk on his face makes Brett like him even less. She throws the journal to him. The book tumbles end over end slowly through the air. Dr. Sims's eyes are fixed on the journal as it sails through the air, and just as it nears his fingers, Dr. Brown races toward him with Brett and Natalie following. The professor plows into Dr. Sims with her shoulder and sends him and the book flying through the air.

Dr. Sims slams on the floor with a thud. Dr. Brown rolls through the collision and lands on her feet.

"Let's get out of here!" Brett yells. She runs ahead with Dr. Brown and Natalie following behind her.

"What about the book?" Natalie asks.

Brett shakes her head as they run out into the hallway. She peers behind Natalie. Dr. Sims is getting to his feet. The sneer on his face sends a shiver up her spine. He glares at her but decides that the prize of having the journal is much more critical than Brett and the others. He walks slowly over to the book and reaches down, picking it up in his delicate hands. A broad smile spreads across his face as he holds it tightly in his hands.

Brett races down the hallway, followed by the others. "Not my dad's book. Now let's go."

They get to the stairs, and Brett throws the door open. She runs up the stairs two at a time. They need to get out of this building as fast as they can. She knows Dr. Sims will be coming after them when he realizes that he has the wrong book.

They rush out into the main hallway, and they hear the door slam open down in the basement. Dr. Sims must have looked in the book and found that it wasn't Dr. Wilson's. They hurry down the hallway, and Brett throws herself through the door at the end of the hall. She stumbles into the humid night air. She pants as she runs toward the Ford Escape. Natalie and Dr. Brown race out of the building after her and run over to the truck. They get inside, and Dr. Brown hurriedly places the key into the ignition and starts the car.

Dr. Sims stumbles out of the doorway just as they pull away.

"GO! GO!" Natalie yells at her mother.

Dr. Brown slams the car into gear and speeds away, leaving Dr. Sims panting beside the road. He watches the Ford Escape speed off down the darkened street with the red taillights growing more faint with each passing second. He turns and slams the door closed.

*****

It is now eleven-thirty, and the roads are empty in Camden, Tennessee. Natalie is looking out the window, searching for the black sedan. In the back seat, Brett is sitting with her legs curled toward her chest, holding her father's book. She stares at it blankly, remembering the words of Dr. Sim's: "Your father was useless to this university." She has never heard her father described as being useless. She knows that Dr. Sims is jealous and angry that discovering Cibola would promote Rock Wilson far above himself. She tells herself that her dad is an exceptional scientist, and somehow he has transferred his book to her. Now it is her job to rescue him.

Brett leans up toward the front seat. Dr. Brown has her eyes fixed on the dark road and doesn't notice Brett. "Dr. Brown?" Brett questions. "I need to go and get Grandpa Jake," she says sternly.

Dr. Brown looks at her with wide eyes. "You can't be serious."

"They have him. I know they do."

"We should call the police, " Dr. Brown says.

"Unfortunately, the bad guy took your phone."

Brett sets her jaw firmly and looks intently in the rear view mirror. "He's coming with us," Brett says. "We're not going back to New Mexico without him." She stares at Dr. Brown through the mirror.

Dr. Brown raises her eyebrows. "Back to New Mexico?"

"They won't stop until they get this book," she says, holding the book up. "I'm not sure how many people we have chasing us, but Dr. Sims said he wasn't one of them. So that means we have others wanting it as well. Who knows how dangerous they are? I'm not leaving Grandpa Jake behind with people like that."

"I don't know, Brett," Dr. Brown implores. "Maybe we should go to the police."

"And tell them what?" Brett responds.

"That your Grandpa is being held captive, and we are running for our lives."

"Dr. Brown. I just want to make sure he is all right."

"This could get dangerous," Dr. Brown replies.

"It is already dangerous, Mom," Natalie says. "Brett needs our help, and I think we should give it to her."

Dr. Brown slows down, coming to a red stoplight. She looks over at Natalie. Natalie looks at her, imploring her to follow through on her promise to help. "We can't leave him," Natalie says.

Brett feels uplifted by the support of her best friend. She realizes that she will need her friend if she plans to succeed in solving the mystery of Cibola. She will need the support and knowledge that Natalie's mother possesses too.

Dr. Brown stares out the window, waiting for the light to turn green. She has a worried expression on her face. She isn't quite sure what to do, but she decides quickly. "All right," she says. The light turns green, and she slowly presses down on the gas pedal. The car gradually moves down the street. "Let's go get Grandpa Jake, find a safe place to rest, and then head to New Mexico."

Natalie lets out a yell. "Okay , Mom! Let's do this."

Brett sits back, smiling. Maybe she will be able to find her dad after all. "Thank you, Dr. Brown," she says.

Dr. Brown nods as she focuses her eyes on the dark streets of Camden.

Brett takes out the worn field book and looks through the brittle pages. The streetlight on the road causes white bands of light to pass over the brown page as she stares down at the words. The words emerge from the book as the glowing light cascades over them. *I rest in a sanctuary that fills my thirst. The walls are golden, and the people are inviting. I wish never to leave this place.* It is signed *Esteban*. This explorer found the city, and he came back. Her dad could come back too.

CHAPTER 8

Go West

The Ford Escape sits on the side street, looking up at Grandpa Jake's farm. Dr. Brown, Natalie, and Brett stare up at the white farmhouse. There is a light on in the upstairs window where Grandpa Jake's bedroom is. They have been watching the house for twenty minutes, waiting to see if anyone else is watching. They haven't seen the black sedan, but the people who are after Cibola are out there—Brett is sure of that.

She takes a deep breath and leans up on the seat between Dr. Brown and Natalie. "No better time than now," she says.

Natalie looks back at Brett nervously. "I guess we can't sit here all night," she says. Brett nods.

Dr. Brown puts the car in drive and leaves the headlights off. The car slowly rolls down the street toward the gravel driveway that leads up to the house. She turns off the asphalt road, and the tires crunch the gravel as the car picks up speed going up the driveway. "In and out," Dr. Brown says.

"Right," Natalie says.

"Keep the car running," Brett says.

"Just be quick," Dr. Brown responds.

The two girls nod. Natalie looks at her hands as they shake uncontrollably. "I'm not scared," she says, looking at Brett.

Brett catches a glimpse of Natalie's hands and feels that her own are quavering far more. She keeps them hidden behind her back as she stares up at the house. Brett is scared out of her mind, but that isn't going to stop her from getting Grandpa Jake out of there. She takes a few deep breaths as the car comes to a stop.

Natalie looks over at Dr. Brown and smiles. The expression tells Dr. Brown that everything will be okay. Her daughter slowly opens the door and hops out. Brett follows, and the girls run up onto the porch. Their feet slam into the wooden planks, creating a thundering sound. They hurry to the door and test the handle; Grandpa Jake at least has locked the door. Brett takes out her key and places it in the lock. She finds herself holding her breath as she turns the key.

Natalie watches as Brett slowly twists the handle. The door creaks open, and the two girls stare into the dark living room. Natalie mouths the words, "I think we should go in." They look at each other and then move stealthily into the house.

Brett's eyes dart from side to side as she enters the living room. Natalie is close behind her as she steps through the room. There isn't anyone waiting for them in the living room or the kitchen. As she nears the steps, Brett spots her old softball bat leaning against the railing. She picks it up and looks at Natalie. Natalie gives her a thumbs-up as they stand looking up the stairs.

Brett peers up the stairs and looks up into the darkness. *Grandpa could have left a light on or something,* she thinks as she steps on the first step. Her weight on the stairs emits a loud creak that shatters the silence of the dark house.

Natalie holds her index finger up to her lips.

"I know," Brett whispers.

They slowly make their way up the steps, being very careful not to make any noise. The bat swings in her hands as she climbs.

At the top of the landing, light cascades out from under the door that leads to Grandpa Jake's room. The two girls walk softly over to the door. Brett holds her breath, trying to hear the faintest sound that could be coming from her grandfather's bedroom. She looks over at Natalie.

Her eyes are wide, and her hands are shaking. Brett gives Natalie the bat and motions with her right hand that she herself will open the door, and she wants Natalie to be ready for anyone coming out. Natalie nods and sets her feet firmly apart like a linebacker and holds the bat high over her head. The bat is swaying rapidly because her arms are shaking so bad.

Satisfied that she can't hear anyone moving in the room, she turns the handle quickly and throws open the door. The light from the room spills out into the hallway. She has to squint because her eyes have become accustomed to the darkness. There are spots in front of her eyes as a large, dark shadow moves toward her. Her mind races, trying to think what to do. She takes a quick step back into the hallway. The shadowy figure is right on top of her, but suddenly the dark form lets out a grunt of pain.

Brett looks up and sees Natalie swinging the bat quickly from right to left, striking the man with deep, thudding blows. The man falls to the ground, and Natalie continues swinging. With each swing there is a clear *thwack* as the metal bat meets the flesh of the attacker. "Get Grandpa Jake, and let's get out of here!" Natalie yells.

Brett hurries into the room, and Grandpa Jake is lying on the bed with a blindfold over his eyes and his hands tied to the headboard. Brett rushes over to him. "Grandpa, we've come to get you." She quickly takes the blindfold off his eyes and starts working on the ropes that have him bound.

Grandpa Jake stares at her in disbelief. "What's going on?" he asks.

Brett struggles with the knots in the ropes. She had never seen knots so tight and uncooperative. Her sweaty fingers fumble over the twine as she finally gets his right hand free.

Natalie yells from the next room, "Hurry up in there!" There is another *thwack*.

Brett gets Grandpa Jake's right hand free and pulls him off the bed.

"What is going on?" he says firmly. "Who is this guy? Need to call the police and have this guy arrested."

"I'll tell you everything as soon as we're out of here," Brett pleads. "But no police."

Grandpa Jake nods and follows Brett out the door. Natalie is sitting on top of the dark figure with a smile on her face and the bat resting on her shoulder. "He must have hit his head. Not bad, huh?" Natalie says.

Lying in a heap below Natalie is the man from the black sedan who has been following Brett. A knot with blood flowing from it sticks out from under his dirty-brown hair. "Hurry," Brett says.

Natalie jumps up and gives the man one more kick before she follows Brett and Grandpa Jake down the stairs.

They hurry through the kitchen and the living room. Brett races out of the house into the stagnant, humid air. She stops on the porch, looking behind her. Grandpa Jake stops at the table just inside the house and grabs an envelope, the "just-in-case envelope" he says, as Brett stares at him incredulously. "Get the bag from the closet," he says, pointing to the closet beside the door. Brett hurries inside and quickly opens the door, pulling out a green army duffel bag. She looks at him questioningly. "This has all our essentials. Clothes, food." Natalie laughs. "A bug-out bag. Nice."

"Always be prepared," Jake says.

"You never know when bad guys will show up at your door," Natalie replies.

Brett throws the bag over her shoulder and follows Grandpa Jake out of the house. Natalie is the last to leave. "Should I close the door?" Brett turns and glares at her. "Right—not important."

They bound down the steps and jump into the waiting car. Dr. Brown waits until all the doors are closed before she thrusts the vehicle into drive and slams her foot down on the gas pedal. Gravel flies out behind the car as the tires try to find grip. She turns the car quickly so she can head down the driveway. As she makes the turn, the dark figure from upstairs jumps off the porch and lands behind the car just as Dr. Brown finally has it going down the driveway.

The figure chases the car, but Dr. Brown presses the pedal to the floor and jumps the dip that connects the driveway to the main road.

The tires squeal as the Ford Escape hits the asphalt, nearly causing the SUV to tip. The car speeds away, and the figure chasing them gets smaller and smaller. Dr. Brown keeps her eyes on the road as she grips the steering wheel tightly.

Natalie is sitting with her knees up on the passenger seat, looking out the back window into the darkness behind them. "Well, that went better than expected," she says. Dr. Brown glances over at her, and Natalie smiles. "You should have seen me lay that guy out. It was great!" Natalie says, beaming. She holds her hand up to Brett with a big smile on her face. "We got that guy."

Brett smiles and slaps her hand. "That's right."

Natalie continues, "Now what are we going to do?"

"We're going to find Cibolaefore they do," Brett says. "We're going to find my dad."

Grandpa Jake is sitting in the back seat next to Brett, looking down at the floor. He tries to make sense of all that has happened since the start of the day. The day has begun precisely as it always does: wake up, feed the animals, have breakfast, make sure the farm is in working order, eat lunch, feed the animals again, do some final chores, eat, and then go to bed.

Unfortunately, Jake has not had the opportunity to finish up the chores, or eat, or go to bed. The insurance man who has visited earlier in the day returned, and that time he wanted something from Jake—he wanted Brett. Jake has not complied with the request, so he was tied up and forced to wait. He still doesn't know why they want Brett.

He looks over at Brett. She is holding a book in her hands, and she looks over at him, giving him an uncomfortable smile. He swallows. "Why are these people after you?" he asks.

Brett holds the book up so that he can see it. "This is Dad's journal," she says. "This is the key to finding a treasure that hasn't been seen in over four hundred years."

Jake stares at her as if she is speaking in a foreign language.

"This is the key to finding Cibola. This is the key to bringing Dad back."

Grandpa Jake closes his eyes and shakes his head. He has heard Rock mention Cibola since his son was a kid. Jake thought he was pretending, but as Rock got older, his obsession with the city continued. The death of Rock is still fresh in Jake's mind. "He's gone, honey," he says. "There's no bringing him back."

Brett reaches over and gently grabs his hand. She smiles at him as tears stream down his face. "Dad is alive," she says. "Trust me. And I know how to find him." She looks down. "Or I *will* know how to find him as soon as I can figure out the clues in his field book."

"*We* will find him," Natalie says.

Grandpa Jake gives Brett a weak smile. "If that is the key to finding Cibola, where do we need to start looking?"

Brett gives him a sheepish grin.

He closes his eyes. "New Mexico," he responds, then opens his eyes.

Brett nods. "New Mexico," she says.

"Sounds like a road trip, Mom!" Natalie cheers.

"Now, wait a minute," Dr. Brown says.

"We have the journal, and we have the magnetoscope," Brett says.

"We have to find Dr. Wilson," Natalie interjects.

"New Mexico here we come," Dr. Brown replies.

"Dr. Brown, I know I can figure out what Dad has written in this book," Brett says, holding it up for her to see. "I need to find him, Dr. Brown. Please."

Dr. Brown drums her fingers on the steering wheel. She is thinking deeply about what has happened in the last twelve hours. It is all just so spectacular, and her analytical, scientific mind is having trouble believing in what has been presented. "This is just u-u-unbelievable," she stammers.

"Yes, it is Mom," Natalie says. "But it is real, and we need to help."

"If Brett says she can solve the clues, I say we give her a shot," Jake says.

Brett stares at him in disbelief. Grandpa Jake has told her to let her father go—be content with his memory. But he is giving her hope that she can find her dad. She hugs him tightly, and he smiles as he pats her on the back. "I should have listened to you, dear," Jake says. "He is out there, and you will find him. And I will help."

Dr. Brown looks through the rearview mirror and sees Brett hugging Grandpa Jake. "Okay," she says.

Natalie cheers. "Yes!" she exclaims. "A road trip. A treasure-hunting road trip, and this time I get to go. This is going to be so awesome."

Dr. Brown glares over at her.

The smile on Natalie's faces fades, and she lowers her eyes. "And we're going to find Dr. Wilson and make everything better for Brett."

Brett stares out the window as the Escape travels down the dark streets of Camden. They pass through the center of town, driving by the large white-columned courthouse. The lights around the building are illuminating the square. This is the first time since her father has disappeared that she is confident he will be found. She smiles as she sits back in her seat and starts to read more of the legend of Cibola that her father has so carefully recorded.

CHAPTER 9

Esteban's Trail

Brett wakes up with a start. Her eyes dart all over the room, searching frantically for what is hidden inside. The shadows in the small square room envelop her. She quickly grabs the book that is sitting on the table next to the bed. She holds it close to her, not wanting to give it up to the dark recesses that appear to be coming for it. Her eyes dart from the door to the small window.

It is still dark outside, but there is a faint glow on the window from the moon. She looks down at the floor, and there beside the bed is her best friend, Natalie. The sight of Natalie sleeping peacefully on the floor snaps her out of the nightmare of people trying to take the book. She breathes deeply and lies back down on the hard pillow.

She looks up at the ceiling and begins to think about all that needs to be done. They have arrived in Houck, Arizona, four days ago. Dr. Brown has insisted that they not return to Thoreau, New Mexico, to begin the search for the city. She is sure that the man in the dark sedan or Dr. Sims and whoever else has been searching for them would start there.

So here they are, staying in a small little house in Houck. After the nightmare, Brett can't seem to find sleep. She reaches down to the floor and feels in the darkness for her bag. She fumbles and grasps until she has the bag's straps in her hands. She pulls the bag onto the bed and feels inside for a light. Her fingers clasp the cylindrical structure of the flashlight, and she turns it on with a click.

With the small beam of light illuminating the bed, Brett opens the book and looks at the maps that are taped on the pages. The Scotch tape has started to brown and pull away from the brittle pages. She finds the meandering lines that indicate the paths that Esteban, De Niza, and Coronado have taken in search of the city. She traces the lines with her fingers, trying to get a feel somehow where it could be.

On the next page, there is a brown leather clipping with a dull hand-drawn map of the southwest portion of the United States. The states of New Mexico and Arizona are rounded in the drawing, looking quite different from the state borders on today's maps. There are also vast canyons depicted on the picture, with arrows indicating the direction of travel. She stares at the caption on the leather page: *I, Estebanico, have found a magnificent, great golden city, and with this map have forever recorded the location.* Brett runs her fingers across the words on the bumpy leather fabric. Her mind races as she tries to pinpoint the area on the map where her father disappeared. The images of the canyon and the haziness in the air come flooding back to her as she stares absently at the leather canvas.

"Something is different," she says aloud. She reaches into her bag and pulls out a topographic map of western New Mexico. The map shows the peaks and valleys, and she quickly finds the location where they were searching for Cibola. She places Esteban's sheet and the topo map side by side and begins tracing the route. She looks from one map to the other and suddenly sits upright. "Esteban was in a different place!" she says breathlessly. "How?"

She moves the leather map under the topo map and flips on the light next to the bed. The room is covered with a dull-white fluorescent glow. She holds the maps up to the light bulb, trying to see a distinct pattern.

Natalie lets out a groan on the floor. "What are you doing?" she asks sleepily.

Brett doesn't respond. Her heart begins to pound as features on the two maps start to match. A smile passes across her face, and she takes a pencil from her bag and draws a large circle on the topographic map. Window Rock Canyon lies right in the center, but it is fifty miles from where they were searching. She has the tip of the pencil in her mouth as she stares at Window Rock Canyon on the map. "How can that be?" she whispers.

Natalie sits up and looks at the maps Brett is holding. "Did you find something? Natalie asks.

Brett looks over at her. "I've found something, but I'm not sure what it is yet."

Natalie squints her eyes, trying to see what Brett is seeing. "I just see a bunch of squiggly lines," Natalie says.

"This is where Estebanico found the city," Brett says, pointing at Window Rock. "But *this* is where *we* found the city."

"Those aren't close together," Natalie responds.

"No, they're not," Brett says.

Natalie lies back on the floor and covers her eyes with her arm. "Could you stare at the dirty old drawing after the sun comes up? I would like to finish sleeping."

Brett stares intently at the maps, not listening. "How would that happen?" she whispers. "How could he be here, and we were there?" She begins chewing on the pencil absentmindedly. A thought enters her mind. "What if the entrance can move? What if it can fluctuate?"

From all the research she has done on electromagnetics, Brett knows that the strengthening and weakening of magnetic fields could account for a phenomenon in which locations in space and time can shift. This could explain the mystery of the disappearing gold city. She drops the pencil as that realization consumes her. "Oh m-m-my," she stammers.

Natalie sits up again, annoyed. "What is it now?" she asks.

Brett looks at her with eyes wide open. "I think I know why the doorway to the city probably isn't in the same location," Brett says.

"Doorway, not in the same place," Natalie sighs. "It's way too early to be thinking about this."

"The door can move because the electromagnetic field that causes it to appear fluctuates, changing its position," Brett says breathlessly.

"I'm going back to sleep," Natalie says, yawning. "Maybe in the morning I will know what you are saying."

Natalie lies back down, and instantly she is breathing deeply, asleep. Brett doesn't notice that her friend is sleeping. Her eyes remain focused on the journal, and a new realization settles in her mind. She runs her hands through her hair the way that her father always does when he is thinking deeply. "Oh dear," she says. "If it moves, how am I going to find it?" She falls back onto her pillows, and the book falls from her hand, landing on the floor with a thud. The sound does not wake Natalie from her heavy slumber, but the weight of reality settles heavily upon Brett's mind and heart. She covers her eyes and presses her palms against her eyeballs.

After a few minutes, Brett slams her fist against the pillows. "I can't," she whispers. "I don't know how to find the door. I can't even begin to figure out how to find the magnetic anomaly that will open the door. And I'm sure I don't know how to predict where it will appear next." Tears stream down her face as she lies on her pillows. The limits of her abilities and knowledge create a massive barrier to finding Cibola. It's what is holding her back from finding her father.

She looks down on the floor at her best friend peacefully sleeping. Brett wants to sleep that deeply without the doubts and fears that keep her awake. She wishes that this were not happening, that her father has not disappeared. That people she doesn't know aren't trying to hurt her. She has invited Natalie into this nightmare, and she feels guilty now for doing that.

Brett begins thinking of walking out into the chilly desert night and leaving Natalie, Dr. Brown, and Grandpa Jake behind. They are much safer away from her. The people looking for the book are not going to stop, and her friends and family are always going to be in danger. "I could give it to those thugs," she says. "Maybe they would let us go home." No. Brett realizes that it's naïve to think that these people would just let them go and return to their normal lives. "What would you do, Dad?" she cries into the darkness.

If her dad were sitting here right now, it would be much better. He would have the answers. He would give her the nuggets of information that would help her with this predicament. She relaxes and in her mind sees her father sitting next to her. She hears his voice as he talks to her about magnetic resonance and how the fields can be amplified, producing a more energetic field of force. The memory is fresh in her mind. When he has spoken about such things, she has not fully grasped what he was saying at the time, but she has loved hearing him talk. His voice has always soothed her, and the memory of his voice comforts her now. "What would you do?" she asks again.

In the silence, she hears his words rushing to her from the darkness that surrounds her: "What does the rock say to you?" That simple question that he always asks in exactly the same way brings a smile to her face. He has trained her for moments like this, and she focuses her mind on the facts. The door to the city moves. The magnetic anomaly changes. Then the words that she said the night before he disappeared enter her mind: "There is a specific time and place when you can access the city."

She sits up quickly and looks around frantically for the book. She grabs it off the floor and pulls it toward her. She flips through the pages quickly, searching for something that she has seen several times but never really analyzed. She finds a page that has her dad's messy handwriting on it. The writing looks like an unrecognizable language scrawled in unrecognizable letters. Fortunately for Brett, she transcribes most of Dr. Wilson's notes: *The anomalies of western New Mexico correlate to the volcanic rock and the sediments found in the rocks. This magnetism originates from deeper in the earth and emanates outward through the sedimentary material. The groundwater system in western New Mexico amplifies the magnetism, creating the perfect conditions for fluctuations in the magnetic field to open doorways into other lands. I believe that Esteban, with guidance from the local Zuni people, was taught how to decipher the points of entry. This is how Esteban found Cibola and possibly the other six cities talked about in the legend.*

Brett's heart beats faster with every sentence she reads. So, the magnetic fields originate from deep in the earth and are made stronger or weaker based on the rock layers above and the amount of water in the ground. She continues reading: *This record shows that if you can follow the groundwater elevations in the area, then the doorways should be present as well.* On the next page, there is a map showing the groundwater system of western New Mexico. As she stares at the picture, an excellent thought enters her mind. She laughs out loud as she turns the pages in the book. Looking at Esteban's map, the route that he took shows that he followed the pathway of groundwater flow.

"The groundwater system is the key," she says.

She turns the page to the map showing Coronado's path. Coronado's and Esteban's routes through New Mexico are nearly identical. The only difference is that Coronado's map shows two courses—Coronado split his forces. She jumps onto the floor. "Coronado found it too!" she exclaims. She races out of the room and hurries toward the couch in the center of the living room.

Grandpa Jake is lying on his back in a deep sleep. His chest rises and falls as Brett runs over to him. She shakes his shoulder lightly. "Grandpa," Brett whispers excitedly. Jake snores loudly, and he rolls on his side with his back to her. She grabs his shoulders and shakes much harder this time, causing his head to move up and down. "Grandpa Jake!"

Jake jumps off the couch, knocking Brett to the floor. His eyes are wide with fear as he looks frantically around the room. He raises his fists in the stance of a boxer as he steps in circles, ready for the man that has caused such fright.

Brett looks up at him from the floor, rubbing her sore elbow. The fall to the floor has caused her to land awkwardly on her side. She slowly gets to her feet with a sigh. With the noise, Jake relaxes and looks down at her. He leans down. "What are you doing on the floor?" he asks.

"You knocked me down."

"I'm sorry, dear," he responds.

She stands up and grabs the book that has fallen beside the couch. "I wanted to show you something. It is important."

Grandpa Jake sits back on the sofa, then lies down, readying himself for sleep once more. "Couldn't it wait until morning?"

Brett shakes her head and sits down forcefully beside him. She moves closer to him, sitting on his legs. Grandpa Jake grimaces in pain.

"No, it can't," she says a little too forcefully. She usually doesn't talk to her grandfather in such a harsh manner.

Jake sits up reluctantly. "All right," he says. "What is it?"

Brett quickly opens the book to the page that shows the map of Esteban's route and Coronado's route. Her heart hammers in her chest, and she tries to find the right words that will enable his understanding. She points to the dark route markers on the map and traces them delicately with her fingers. "This is Esteban's route when he found Cibola, and this is the route Coronado took. Look at the similarities. They are almost identical."

Jake stares down at the map, watching her fingers intently as they trace the lines. He rubs the stubble on his chin with his right hand as he looks up at her. "Coronado followed the route Friar de Niza followed when he saw the city," Jake says.

Brett nods. Her grandfather looks down and points to the area on the map where the two routes diverge. "What happened here?" he asks.

She smiles and looks at him excitedly. "That is where Coronado split his forces."

Grandpa Jake sits back and rubs his chin. "Now, why would he do that?" he asks.

"I think that he split his forces because he found the entrance but didn't want to share its location," she says breathlessly.

"You believe he found it?" Jake asks.

"Dad believed he found it, and I believe he found it." She flips the page to the map showing the groundwater elevations for the western portion of New Mexico. "This is how Dad found the city, Grandpa." She points to the groundwater elevation map and then hurriedly flips back to the routes of Coronado and Esteban. "Notice that the groundwater elevations are very high along the route," she says.

He looks down and scrutinizes the maps. "Those elevations correlate to the route," Brett continues. He glances up at her.

She smiles broadly. "And then there is this," she says as she shows him the magnetic anomaly map. The high levels of magnetism are present on the same grid as the groundwater elevations and the path.

Grandpa Jake wipes his eyes with his left hand. "He figured it out, didn't he?" Jake asks. Brett nods and smiles. Grandpa Jake smiles back at her with tears glistening his eyes. "You figured it out too." He places his arm around her shoulder and pulls her toward him. "I hope he is there," he says.

Brett allows her grandfather's hug to swallow her. It gives her peace that he is always there for her and watches out for her. It also raises her spirits that he finally believes that her dad is alive, and she knows how to find him. She looks up at him. "Now, all we have to do is figure out where the doorway is going to be."

"Figure out?" he asks. "I thought you knew where it was."

"I know it exists," she responds. "But I don't know where it is going to be."

"You don't know where it is going to be?"

"The door moves, Grandpa."

"It moves?"

"The fluctuations in the magnetic field cause the doorway to shift."

Grandpa Jake closes his eyes and shakes his head. "I don't understand."

She shows him a page in the book that talks about the amplification of the magnetic field because of the vast reservoirs of groundwater. "Dad found that groundwater amplifies earth's magnetic field, and as the magnetic field fluctuates, the severity of the forces the field exerts can be enhanced or reduced," she says.

Grandpa Jake shakes his head. "I'm a simple farmer, dear," he says.

She holds the book up so that he can see the image. The expression on her face is determined. "We follow this, and we find the doorway. We follow this, and we find Dad."

"But—"

"Dr. Brown will help me figure out where it's going to be next." Brett smiles a smile that spreads across her face. Her eyes dance as she stares at Grandpa Jake.

"I don't doubt you will find him," he says. "You are just like your dad."

Brett's heart leaps wildly in her chest. She has always wanted to be like her father, and at this moment, she feels that she is finally living up to being Rock Wilson's daughter.

*****

Brett cannot get back to sleep after talking to her grandfather. He has convinced her to wait until morning to present her new information to Dr. Brown. She has agreed, but she spends the rest of the night listening to Natalie breathing loudly in her deep sleep. She wants to get out and find the doorway, but stumbling around in the New Mexico backcountry in the dark would be difficult, even if you know exactly where you are going. She does not know where the door might appear, but she will find it.

She lies back on her pillows, staring up at the white tiles on the ceiling. She shines the dull beam of the flashlight toward the ceiling. The tiles are yellowed for some reason. She thinks about how the white tiles could turn this gross shade of yellow. As she thinks of a logical explanation, she counts the small holes that are in the tiles. She makes it to 405 when she finally stops. She glances at the clock, and the green numbers flash across her eyes—6:00.

Brett hops out of bed and nearly lands on Natalie's head. She races out of the room and into the living room. Grandpa Jake eyes her with irritation as Brett barges into the room. He surveys her face carefully as she walks by the couch. "Didn't get back to sleep, did you?"

Brett stops and gives him a crooked smile. "Why do you say that?"

"Well, you reluctantly agreed to let Dr. Brown sleep. So I'm guessing that you put your head on your pillows and thought about how to find the anomaly that opens the doorway to Cibola," Jake says directly.

"For your information, I analyzed why the tiles on the ceiling are a disgusting yellow color," she replies.

"Oh," Jake responds.

"Time to show Dr. Brown what we have." Brett walks through the living room with a single-minded purpose. The path of Esteban is ahead of them, and she needs Dr. Brown to pinpoint the exact location. That will allow them to enter the golden city of Cibola. Her steps become faster as she moves through the kitchen and stands at a closed door. It is odd to have a bedroom off the kitchen, but this house has one. Maybe the person who built it enjoyed eating in the middle of the night. Brett herself has snuck plenty of chocolate-chip muffins from their kitchen at home, but she was much farther from the source than this bedroom.

She takes a deep breath as she stares at the closed door. She hopes that Dr. Brown is fully awake behind the door. She does not want to wake her up, but it is time to get out there. Brett knocks lightly on the door. She waits patiently for any response from the other side of it. The seconds tick by endlessly as Brett waits for Dr. Brown. She decides that she will try again. She raps harder this time on the door, and the sound of the knock engulfs the room. Brett stands back, anticipating Dr. Brown's emergence from the bedroom.

After a minute of waiting, Brett starts to get a little annoyed. *Doesn't Dr. Brown know that we are racing against unknown villains in our pursuit of finding Cibola first? Doesn't she know that we have to get there first?* She grits her teeth and steps up to the door a third time. Brett doesn't notice that Grandpa Jake is right behind her. She gets ready to rap on the door again when he grabs her hand. He holds his index finger to his lips. She doesn't understand what Grandpa Jake is asking. "She's not coming out," Brett says tersely.

"Maybe there is a reason why Dr. Brown isn't answering," Jake replies.

Brett shakes her head. Fear quickly envelops her. Her chest feels tight, and she starts taking short breaths. She has felt this way when the black sedan chased them through Camden. What if those men are here in this small town?

Grandpa Jake sees the worry on her face and motions toward the door. Brett watches, and he grabs the handle lightly and starts to turn the knob. He slowly pulls the door outward toward them. Grandpa Jake peers inside. Brett's heart is beating fast, and her breathing comes out in short bursts as she waits for the word that everything is as it should be.

As Grandpa Jake opens the creaking door, there is an audible gasp from the bedroom. "What is it?" Dr. Brown says, frightened.

Jake steps into the room, followed by Brett. Dr. Brown is sitting at a table with her computer out with her hand placed on her chest. There are aerial images of the western portion of New Mexico up on the screen. Her field book is open, and she is holding a ruler and a compass.

"We thought something happened to you," Grandpa Jake says.

"We thought those men found us!" Brett exclaims.

Dr. Brown breathes a sigh of relief, and her arm falls to her side. "You two nearly gave me a coronary," she says.

Brett walks over and stares at the images on the screen. Jake's voice booms a little too loudly in the room. "You didn't answer when we knocked."

Dr. Brown looks at the screen, saying nothing.

Jake presses, "We thought something happened to you."

The professor glances up at him and shrugs. "I'm still not accustomed to being chased all over the country," she replies. There, beside the desk, is a pair of headphones. She picks them up, showing them to Jake. "I listen to music when I want to concentrate," she says.

Jake shakes his head, turns, and walks out the door. His voice resounds loudly from the other room. "I'm making breakfast, and I expect everyone to eat!" he yells. "I suspect we're going out into the country to look for Esteban or Coronado, so we need to be well fed." The sound of Jake loudly opening the cabinets and pulling things out can be heard inside the small bedroom.

Dr. Brown looks up at Brett. "I think I found how the magnetic anomaly originates," she says. Brett lays her dad's field book on the desk, and Dr. Brown looks down at it intently. Her eyes are keenly focused on the maps that are in front of her.

"Bedrock layers plus groundwater levels equal amplification of magnetism," Brett says.

Dr. Brown nods her head in agreement. She turns the page in the book, looking closely at the maps and figures on the pages that follow. The data shows complex math formulas that Brett does not understand. That is why Brett has come to her room. "This shows the intensity of the field and how it resonates through the metallic portions of the rock. This one describes how the water column amplifies the signal, as well," Dr. Brown says carefully.

Brett surveys the formulas and nods her head as if she genuinely understands the complexity of what Dr. Brown is telling her. Brett is a very bright eleven-year-old girl, but math at this level still causes her brain to hurt.

Dr. Brown continues looking at the numbers, her fingers tapping lightly on the table to the tune of a song. Brett can see that her mind is processing information very quickly. Quickly, Dr. Brown picks up the ruler and compass and begins marking the map that is in front of her. Dr. Brown's eyes dart from the book to the computer screen and then to the map. She is mumbling to herself. Brett stares in amazement as Dr. Brown works feverishly. A smile spreads across Dr. Brown's face.

"Dr. Brown, I believe we can find the location of where the anomaly will appear next," Brett says. "I think we should head out there today."

Dr. Brown is still drawing on her map and adding calculations so that the anomalies protrude from the image. She continues muttering as each anomaly emerges on the screen. It is as if she hasn't heard Brett.

Brett clears her throat. "Dr. Brown." The professor holds up her hand and types the last few figures into the computer. The screen lights up with red and orange colors.

Dr. Brown turns and smiles. "That is our location," she says. "Crown Point is our spot. That should be where we'll find the city." Brett stares at the screen. That is where her dad is, and she is almost there.

Dr. Brown drops the ruler and compass. She claps her hands together and looks over at Brett. "The figures tell the tale," Dr. Brown says. She points to the map on the table, and Brett leans over, looking at the circles that she has drawn with the compass. Straight lines are crossing the circles in thirty-, forty-five-, and sixty-degree angles, but Brett shakes her head, not understanding.

Dr. Brown points to the circle around Thoreau. "This is where Dr. Wilson disappeared," Dr. Brown says. She traces the line through the next ring. "And *this* is where the anomaly appeared a few weeks ago." Dr. Brown has her finger on the map where Cuba, New Mexico, is located.

Brett traces the line farther to the north, towards the next circle that has two long lines inside it, forming an X. "That's where it's going to be?" Brett asks.

Dr. Brown nods. "We need to hurry," she says. "If my calculations are correct, the city should become visible two days from now." She looks at her watch. "At roughly 7:30 a.m."

Brett stares down at the map, lost in thought. Her dad will be there. He will be pleased that she has found the city just like he did. She looks at the X. It is a little west of Dixon, New Mexico. "X marks the spot," Brett utters.

Dr. Brown agrees. "X marks the spot."

Brett has looked at the Esteban map and the Coronado map what seems like thousands of times. She has never guessed they would be that far east, but the routes each man took led precisely to each location.

Brett begins to wonder if these two men, without modern instruments, understood how to find the city of gold. They had to understand the complexity of finding it. Maybe they had some understanding that contemporary people do not have. It is probably knowledge that the native peoples have had. Brett becomes overwhelmed by the truth that the native peoples have known far more about earth and its complexities than people today.

Brett glances at Dr. Brown, who is drumming on the desk again. "Time to follow Esteban to Cibola," Brett says.

Dr. Brown nods. "I have a feeling we will see some familiar faces before we get there," she replies.

Brett looks at her sternly. She isn't going to let those men or the vile Dr. Sims get in her way. Brett is determined, and she will fight anyone who blocks her. Brett will find the city, and she will bring her dad back home. The route of Esteban will bring her to the golden city. That is a fact.

CHAPTER 10

Coronado's Ghost

The air is light and warm as they bring the last of the bags out of the house. The orange glow of the sun is starting to heat up the brown gravel in the driveway. The wind kicks up some dust that dances across the driveway. Brett finds the heat in Arizona much easier to acclimate to than the hot, humid air in Camden. At this time of morning back home, your clothes would already be sticking to you.

Grandpa Jake steps out of the house, carrying a large bag that smells of freshly cooked biscuits and bacon. "This is the last of it," he says as he throws the bag in the back seat.

Dr. Brown climbs into the dusty Escape and instinctively buckles her seat belt. She closes the door, sending dust particles flying into the warm morning air. Brett and Natalie hop in the back. There is an air of excitement buzzing through the back seat. Brett has felt the same energy the morning that they set out for Cibola a few months ago. This must be what her dad felt: the delight, the pride, and the fear. She grips the bag tightly in her sweaty hands. The field journal inside the bag has brought her this far, so she holds it tightly.

Grandpa Jake sticks his head through the passenger-side window. "Everybody ready?" he asks.

Dr. Brown nods as she grips the steering wheel tightly.

"Get in, Grandpa Jake," Natalie beckons. "We have a treasure to find."

Jake flashes a caring glance at Brett. She stares back at him, smiling. The smile is a sign to him that she is all right. Brett knows that Grandpa Jake is afraid of the others who are searching for the city. He is fearful that they will hurt her. He closes his eyes slowly and climbs into the seat.

"Next stop—Cibola!" Natalie cries.

"Next stop—Cibola," Brett says stoically.

Dr. Brown starts the SUV and pulls out of the driveway. The dust billows out behind the car as they near the main road. The trip of Houck to Dixon should take around four and a half hours if they take the main roads, and that is what they are doing. Dr. Brown turns onto I-40 and heads east into the blazing sunlight. The gold rings around the sun remind Brett of the lasting image she has of Cibola: the glowing oranges and yellows are reflecting off the walls of the golden city. It is real, and in a little more than four hours, she will be standing among those golden walls finally.

*****

Dr. Brown drives down State Road 68, northwest of Dixon. She keeps glancing in the rearview mirror. Brett can see the mixture of worry and excitement etched on her tired face. Brett is sure that she looks the same way, but the fear of being found has diminished. She looks out the window and can see Black Mesa Mountain looming in the distance. The tabletop mountain, with its contrasting greens and browns, is a magnificent sight. Brett thinks that under different circumstances, she would like to stop and look at the rocks, but today they are heading farther to the northeast.

They continue east on 68, passing the intersection of Highway 75. Everyone in the SUV remains silent. The close proximity to the city keeps their thoughts on finding the treasure, and it also keeps them away from idle conversation. Even Natalie finds it difficult to speak.

She stares out the window, waiting patiently for the final turn toward the homestretch.

After ten more minutes of riding, Dr. Brown checks the coordinates on the GPS she has on the dash. She looks ahead. Dr. Brown slows down and gradually turns off the paved road onto a dirt road. The dirt billows up behind the car as Dr. Brown steers upward through the scrub plants and rock outcrops. The travelers continue upward in elevation as Highway 68 begins to recede behind them. "Almost there," she says.

Grandpa Jake looks back at the two girls. "Stay safe out there. We don't know what we will encounter," Jake says sternly.

Brett smiles. "We will be all right."

"I'm sure Rock thought the same thing," Jake says.

Brett lowers her eyes. She was there. She wasn't near her father when he disappeared, but the humming that the magnetic field created still rings in her ears.

Natalie sits up high in her seat, gripping the headrest. The dirt road curves to the left as it goes around a pinnacle. Dr. Brown stops the SUV at the top of the incline. There in front of them is the most scenic landscape Brett has ever seen. The tall mountains in the distance cast blue and gray shadows over the entire landmass. Closer to their position, the canyons and ridges alternate in a distinctive pattern.

The orange and brown rocks of the canyons remind Brett of the canyons where the first expedition had gone. Her heart begins racing as she climbs out of the Escape for a better view. Down in one of these canyons is where Cibola is hiding. Her breath comes in short bursts as she grips the handles of her bag tightly. She takes a deep, refreshing breath, trying to calm her nerves.

"You ready to do this?" Dr. Brown asks.

"Absolutely," Brett responds.

"Woohoo!" Natalie yells.

Dr. Brown opens the back of the SUV and takes out her pack with all her gear. She quickly slings it over her shoulder. Grandpa Jake has his bag with their food, and he walks up beside Brett. He places his brown, wrinkled hand on her shoulder. "I'm proud of you," he says.

Brett looks up at him. Her eyes are dancing around with excitement. "I can't wait to see it again," she says.

Brett opens her bag and takes out the magnetoscope, then turns it on. A humming sound comes from the machine, followed by a series of beeps and blips. After a few seconds, the device is silent. She holds it in her right hand, looking at the others. "Hope this thing works," Brett says.

Dr. Brown closes the doors on the SUV and pulls out her field book. She opens it to the center and stares at the map that she has taped inside. The large concentric circles and the large X marked in dark ink jump out from the page. She looks out at the rugged hills toward the northwest. Cerro Azul, Moreno, and Colorado stand like sentinels in the waning afternoon sun. She scans the horizon and pinpoints the proper trajectory of the descent into the canyon. "Thirty degrees off this straight-line trajectory should get us to the bottom and moving toward the anomaly," Dr. Brown says, pointing away from the peaks to the west.

Brett, Natalie, and Jake stare off into the distance where Dr. Brown indicates. "Looks a little hairy," Jake says as he scratches his chin.

"Don't worry, Grandpa Jake. Mom said Brett went off a cliff much steeper than this one the last time," Natalie says.

Jake shoots a concerned look at Brett as she picks up her bag and throws it over her shoulder. She walks toward the rocky canyon wall with the magnetoscope in one hand and the field book in the other. Natalie runs after her, leaving Jake standing with Dr. Brown. "I guess we are doing this," he says.

Dr. Brown nods determinedly and strides off toward the two girls.

Jake stares at the three females walking ahead of him. How extraordinary it is to have an eleven-year-old girl, her friend, and a female geologist leading such a remarkable expedition. This expedition into the mysterious past has generated tons of interest over the years, and here they are on the verge of a discovery. Jake smiles as he walks off toward the sheer canyon wall. His confidence builds as he watches each of their figures start the rapid descent down into the rocky canyon.

After an hour of walking, Brett stops along the ledge leading down into the valley. She peers down into the darkness. The sun is venturing farther to the west, leaving the valley below shielded from the sun's rays. She squints her eyes, trying to make out the features that are ahead of them, but the shadows are covering the floor of the valley.

She takes a bottle of water out of her bag and takes a large gulp. The heat on the rocky ledge is intense. The rocks have absorbed sunlight all day, and now they are radiating that sunlight back into the air. The temperature is stifling, and the cold water feels refreshing on her parched lips and tongue. She smacks her lips and places the top slowly on the bottle.

"How much farther do you think it is?" Natalie asks as she takes a drink too.

"An hour maybe," Brett says as she surveys the brown rocks along the canyon trail.

"Oh good," Natalie responds. "I thought you were going to tell me it is going to be another three or four. That would not be all right."

Grandpa Jake and Dr. Brown are behind, standing against the rock wall, looking at the two girls. They are talking in a light whisper. Natalie points at them. "You can say it in front of us, you know."

Dr. Brown yells back, "We are discussing where we should make camp tonight!"

"Oh," Natalie says. "You mean we're staying out here tonight?"

Brett glances at her and grimaces, knowing that the harshness of the environment could impact their comfort—and their sleep.

Natalie shakes her head. "I thought we were sleeping in the car."

Brett shakes her head, laughing. "Don't worry. You only have to worry about coyotes, scorpions, and rattlesnakes."

Natalie looks at her with her eyes wide. "Is that all?" she responds. She pulls the straps on her pack tight and starts walking down the path toward the valley floor. "I can do this," she says as she walks away.

Brett wipes the sweat from her sun-drenched face and watches as Natalie strides off down the narrow trail. Suddenly, Natalie's leg buckles as she steps on a loose rock in the middle of the path. She falls forward and, as she tries to regain her balance, steps on another loose rock that slides down the edge of the trail into the valley below.

Dr. Brown lets out a loud gasp. "No!" she screams.

Brett watches as Natalie is teetering on the edge between the trail and the valley below. "Natalie!" she yells.

Natalie looks at her, the fear of falling etched on her face, and then she tumbles over the edge.

Dr. Brown screams as Natalie disappears from the trail.

Brett continues forward, fearful that they have lost Natalie. She hopes that somehow, Natalie is holding on. Brett can hear Dr. Brown screaming behind her as she runs forward. "Natalie! Are you there?" Brett screams.

Brett hurries over to the ledge where Natalie vanished. She steps out quickly and looks down, fearful that she will see her friend's mangled body lying at the base of the rocky canyon wall. She peers over and, to her surprise, sees that Natalie has managed to grab and hold on to a long orange slab of rock.

Natalie gazes up at her friend. She has blood flowing down her sweat-soaked face. "I was able to hold on," she says with a laugh.

Brett turns around and yells at Dr. Brown and Grandpa Jake, who are sprinting toward her. "She's okay."

Brett looks down at where Natalie is gripping the rock with both hands. The lower half of her body is dangling in the air. Brett looks around, seeing if she can find a way to get Natalie back to the ledge where the rest of them are standing.

Natalie laughs loudly as she watches Brett trying to figure out what to do. "Don't mind me," Natalie says. "I will just hang out down here until you guys figure out what to do."

Dr. Brown finally makes it to the ledge. She peers over and sees Natalie grasping the rock face. "Oh. Hey, Mom!" Natalie yells. "Bet you didn't think this would happen. Did you?" Brett turns and looks for something she can use to get to Natalie.

Grandpa Jake steps to the ledge, and he quickly throws his bag down on the ground and rummages through the contents. "Hold on a little longer, Natalie!" he yells. He throws the sandwiches and the water bottles on the ground. He lets out a yell as he pulls a coiled-up rope out of the bag.

Brett sees the rope. She quickly grabs the end and begins lowering it down to her friend. "Grab it!" she yells.

Natalie nods as the line slowly draws closer to her hands.

Grandpa Jake rushes to the other side of the rocky trail with the rope wrapped around his waist. Brett glances at him as he sets his feet at shoulder-width apart and braces himself against the rock wall. Brett looks down at Natalie as the rope slowly moves closer to her.

"Just a little farther!" Natalie screams.

Dr. Brown is frantically calling to her, "It's okay! We're going to pull you up."

Natalie looks down at the valley floor, and her head begins to swim. "I shouldn't have done that," she says. As Natalie peers into the shadows of the valley below, her heartbeat quickens as a glinting silver glow flashes brightly from the canyon below her. She looks harder, trying to figure out what is down there, aside from a fall of sixty feet. The glinting light illuminates the shadows, revealing a tall figure with a black mustache and a silver helmet. "Whoa!" She gasps at the sight, but the man below her does not appear to hear her. His head remains firmly fixated on the rocky canyon floor.

Suddenly the rope hits her face, and she looks up quickly. "Grab the rope!" Dr. Brown yells.

Natalie looks down again. The glowing man with the silver helmet has vanished. "Did you guys see that?" she asks.

"Just grab the rope so we can get you up here!" Brett yells.

Natalie ignores the rope, and again she looks down into the valley. The only things down at the rocky bottom are shadows and rocks. Natalie searches a few seconds for the mysterious figure, and when she doesn't see him, she reaches up and grabs the rope.

Brett and Grandpa Jake pull with all their strength, and Natalie begins moving up the rock face. Dr. Brown hurries over and grabs the rope and begins pulling with the others. Natalie's dirty face appears over the ledge as Brett, Jake, and Dr. Brown pull. Dr. Brown drops the rope and hurries over to Natalie. She falls on the ground and grabs her daughter's arms and pulls Natalie onto the path. "Are you okay?" Dr. Brown says through her hysterical sobs.

Natalie is lying facedown on the trail, breathing deeply.

Dr. Brown falls on top of her, hugging and kissing her.

"I'm never doing that again," Natalie says.

"I don't think I'm going to *let* you do that again. I should have been more careful," Dr. Brown says in a strained voice.

Brett and Jake watch as they hug and cry on the dusty trail. Brett can't take her eyes away from her friend. Natalie is in danger because of her. Brett wants her to be here helping, but Natalie has almost died. Brett grits her teeth and looks down the trail that leads into the valley below. She must continue. She must find her father. Dr. Brown has helped her locate the city, and now the professor's job is finished. She can take Natalie and return to Camden, where both of them will be safe. It is the book the men are coming for, after all, and with Natalie and Dr. Brown back home, Brett won't have to worry about their safety any longer.

Brett wipes a tear away from her right eye and walks over to Natalie. She leans down and pats her on the back. "Glad you're all right," she says.

Natalie looks up and tries to smile at her, but it appears more like a grimace. There are cuts on her face from the rocks that she slid on, and Dr. Brown is trying to wipe some of the blood away. Dr. Brown looks over at Brett. "I think we should stop this," Dr. Brown says.

After this near catastrophe, Brett has known that Dr. Brown would be ready to stop. It is her daughter who almost fell to her death.

Brett nods. "Yeah. I think that is probably best. I don't want anyone getting hurt."

"I'm sorry," Dr. Brown says. "I know it's a chance to find Rock, but I can't risk Natalie. We should go back to Houck and alert the state police. They did the original investigation."

"I am finishing this, Dr. Brown," Brett says. "We're here."

"I can't let you."

"I understand, Dr. Brown. I don't want anything bad happening to anyone," Brett responds. Brett picks up her bag and slings it over her shoulder. She takes out the magnetoscope and looks at the dial, satisfied that it still is going to lead her to Cibola. She starts down the trail. Grandpa Jake watches as Brett walks determinedly away. He has seen that focused look in Rock, and he knows that she will not stop until she finds him. He stuffs the rope from the rescue in his bag and walks quickly after her.

Natalie looks up as Brett moves away down the trail. "She can't leave without us," Natalie says to Dr. Brown.

Dr. Brown is still cleaning the blood from Natalie's face and arms. "We're calling the police like we should have done a long time ago," Dr. Brown asserts. "And then we're going home."

Natalie stares down the trail. She pushes Dr. Brown's hands away and tries to get up on her feet, but she falls back onto her stomach. "Brett! Brett!" she yells.

Brett can hear the yells coming from behind her. She wipes tears from her eyes as she continues down the incline into the valley. She refuses to turn around. Only Brett searching with Jake is best for everyone. Her feet crunch on the rocky path as the sun fades away behind the hills to the west. The darkness of her descent begins to envelop her. Brett breathes deeply as she continues down the trail into the black shadows below. She is alone now with Grandpa Jake, and maybe it is better this way.

Dr. Brown tries to hold Natalie down on the dusty, rocky path. Natalie struggles to her feet and spreads her legs so that she doesn't fall again. "You're not leaving me behind!" she yells.

Dr. Brown hurries to her feet and tries to put her arms around Natalie. Her daughter glares at her and points her bloody index finger at Brett. "We're not letting her do this alone," she says.

"We are getting the police and going home," Dr. Brown replies.

"We came this far," Natalie protests. "And she needs us."

"It's over, Natalie," Dr. Brown says firmly. "We're getting you home."

"I'm not going," Natalie says.

Natalie takes an uneasy step down the rocky pathway. She stumbles but doesn't fall. She fights back the tears as she walks. Sharp pain shoots through her legs with every step, but she isn't going to stop. "Brett!" she yells. "We're finishing this together."

Brett continues walking, not wanting to turn around. It is better just to leave.

Natalie takes three more painful, stumbling steps. Dr. Brown rushes up behind her, trying to steady Natalie on her feet.

Natalie vividly remembers the bearded man she saw down in the canyon. She grits her teeth. "I saw someone down there when I was hanging off the cliff. He had a black mustache and a silver helmet. He didn't look like someone from our time!" Natalie calls breathlessly to Brett. The words crash over Natalie like the massive boulders that have fallen into the canyon below. She has seen someone. Natalie has seen someone wearing a silver helmet. In her mind, she sees the picture of Francisco Coronado with his black manicured mustache and silver conquistador helmet. A cold chill goes down her spine, and she stops dead in her tracks. "Who do you think it is?" Natalie yells.

"You saw someone? Down there?" Dr. Brown says.

"Yes, and I didn't imagine it."

Brett turns and looks back up the slope. Grandpa Jake is about twenty yards from her, stepping gingerly on the uneven ground. He is halfway between Brett and Natalie, and his brow furrows at the description Natalie gives.

"Sounds like Coronado," Brett says.

Natalie looks at her with her mouth open as if she can't believe it. "What?!" Natalie yells.

"It sounds like you saw Coronado," Brett says.

"He's dead, right?" Natalie responds.

"For over four hundred years," Brett replies.

Natalie looks at her mother with a worried look on her scratched and bloody face. Dr. Brown is pale, and her hands shake as she tries grabbing Natalie. "Our job is—"

Natalie looks at her sternly. "Mom, Dr. Wilson wouldn't make me go alone if it were *you* who was lost out there. So we're not letting Brett go alone."

Dr. Brown looks at Brett and then back at Natalie. "You're right."

Brett walks toward them, and she has the field book open, turning the pages quickly. She knows what she's looking for, and she finds it quickly. She walks by Jake without acknowledging him. Her focus is on the image and making sure that who Natalie saw was indeed Coronado. If it is true—this whole expedition is taking on a new twist. They are now finding people that were supposed to have died hundreds of years ago. This is something unheard of.

Brett walks up to Natalie and holds the field book up where she can see it. There on the page is a copy of a painting depicting Francisco Vázquez de Coronado y Luján. His pointed chin is covered by wisps of dark hair. His dark eyes are peering out stoically, as if the image captured his first sight of the city. "Is this the guy you saw in the valley?" Brett asks.

Natalie looks at the picture carefully with her nose wrinkled. She glances up at Brett. "Could be. I was dangling off a cliff, so it is hard to say," she says.

Brett closes the book and looks down the trail toward Grandpa Jake. He has a scowl on his face, unlike any expression that Brett has ever seen. She is sure that he thinks they should get to the SUV and head out of town, but Jake surprises her. He points down the trail. "We need to make camp at the bottom before nightfall," he says.

Natalie grabs Brett's arm. "We're sleeping down there with the ghost of Coronado or whoever that guy is?" Natalie asks.

"Ghosts aren't real," Dr. Brown says.

"I saw one," Natalie responds. "So they are."

Brett places the book into her bag and sets the magnetoscope carefully on top of the book, then zips the bag closed. "Grandpa is right. We need to get to the bottom before it gets dark," Brett says. She begins walking down the path.

When she makes it to Grandpa Jake, he steps beside her. He pats her on the shoulder with his big, strong hands. "One step closer," Jake says proudly.

Brett smiles at him as they walk down the rocky path. "We will be in Cibola tomorrow," she says. "I can't wait to see Dad."

Natalie watches Brett and Jake descending the sloping trail toward the valley. She looks at Dr. Brown and shrugs her shoulders. "You have to say this little adventure has it all: bad guys chasing us, lost treasure, and now ghosts of Spanish conquistadors," Natalie says. "It doesn't get much better than this." She hobbles down the slope toward her best friend.

Dr. Brown stares at her in disbelief.

"It's getting dark," Natalie says. "You coming?"

Dr. Brown shakes her head and falls in line behind Natalie. "Yeah, I'm coming," Dr. Brown says. "For the record, ghosts don't exist. I know this because I'm a scientist."

Natalie laughs. "You're a geologist. That's not a scientist," she says with a loud shout of laughter.

Dr. Brown relaxes for the first time since seeing Natalie fall over the edge, and she laughs too.

CHAPTER 11

Shining City on the Hill

The valley of the canyon is absent of any light except the flashes from the headlamps that Brett, Jake, Natalie, and Dr. Brown are wearing. The beams of lights pass along the vertical rock face and show the magnitude of the distance above them. Natalie slumps down against the yellowish-orange rock. She is breathing hard and wipes sweat away from her scratched face. Dr. Brown kneels over her, checking the cuts on her arms and face.

"It's fine, Mom," Natalie protests.

Brett looks into the darkness that has filled the canyon floor, and a cold chill flows up her back. Her headlamp beam becomes enveloped by the darkness about six feet ahead of her. She strains her eyes, but she can't even make out the direction of the dusty path. She knows it moves off to the northeast, but without light, moving farther would be dangerous.

Jake walks over to her and touches her shoulder. "I think this spot looks as good as any," he says.

She nods, agreeing, and places her bag down on the gravel-strewn ground. Wherever they sleep down here probably will not be the most comfortable place. The gravel poking a person in the back all night is going to make sleep difficult.

Grandpa Jake places his bag on the ground and begins rummaging inside. He pulls out a few of the wrapped sandwiches and hands them to Brett, Natalie, and Dr. Brown. "We should eat something to keep our strength up," he says.

Grandpa Jake takes his sandwich and rips the wrapping off quickly, then, like a hungry animal, devours it in two bites. He wipes his mouth with the back of his hand and sits down. "That's good," he says. He sits with his back resting on his pack and pulls a tarnished old silver harmonica from his pocket. He begins softly playing a sweet tune that is soft and enchanting. The music is quiet and soothing, and it barely leaves the circle of their encampment.

Dr. Brown drops down beside Natalie, unwraps a sandwich, and hands it to her. They eat as they listen to soft music. The music takes them away from the memory of Natalie almost falling into this very canyon a few hours before. The two of them stare off into the darkness as they eat, allowing the music to bathe them in its calming mood.

Brett watches her best friend and her mother. She is glad that they are still here with her in this dark, depressing place. Brett knows that in the morning, the darkness will be gone, and it will be replaced by the bright sunlight that will bake this canyon well above one hundred degrees. She hopes they can find the entrance to the city long before that happens.

Brett looks at the sandwich. The excitement of the expedition pushes the thought of eating out of her mind and she stuffs the little meal into her bag beside the silent magnetoscope. She looks at the narrow machine with apprehension. Brett hopes that it works as well as the one Dr. Mies brought on the first expedition. As she sits in the darkness, the fears of it not working start closing in on her. It feels like a massive weight is sitting on her chest. She takes a deep breath. *It has to work*, she says to herself. *Dad's worked. This one will work. Trust yourself, Brett. Be confident in what you know.*

With those words permeating her mind, she relaxes and enjoys the music. A smile spreads across her face, and she takes out her dad's field book. She thumbs through the brownish-yellow pages. The maps of Coronado, Esteban, and the others pass as she turns the pages of Esteban's diary. She settles on the page that is marked by a baseball card.

The card is of George Brett, the Kansas City Royals' greatest player. He is standing ready to field the ball at third base.

Brett picks the card up and looks at it absently. George Brett is her dad's favorite player, after whom she's named. As she stares at the determined face of George Brett, she remembers the night before her dad has disappeared. They talked about the excitement of discovery, but they also just talked with each other. She remembers that they listened to a Royals game that night. That is something that she wishes she were doing now. She could have brought a radio and listened to a game. The Royals are playing somewhere, and it would be pleasant to hear.

Tears begin forming in her eyes as she thinks back to that night. The melodic music also causes her heart to feel heavy. The doubts are in her, but she forces herself to believe. "I will find you, Dad," she mutters to herself. "We will listen to many games together. I can't wait." She closes her eyes, and a tear streaks across her face. She returns the card to the book and lies back on her bag. She holds on to the journal so tightly that her fingers are white.

Brett allows the soft music to flow over her, and she begins to drift into the waiting arms of restful sleep. It has been a long day, and tomorrow will be much longer. She lets herself drift away into the blackness, and soon the sound of the harmonica is fading into the distance.

Grandpa Jake glances over at her as she lies motionless. He plays softer, and the melody of the song is lulling. Jake glances at Dr. Brown, and she is holding Natalie in her arms as Natalie sleeps. He takes a deep breath and continues playing, and the music fills the canyon with beauty and hope for the morning that is coming.

*****

Brett jumps from her sound sleep and searches frantically around her. The embers from the campfire glow red, and small rays of red light flicker in the darkness. Her fingers fumble frantically around her as she feels for a source of light. Daylight must still be hours away, and something out in the night has brought her out of her slumber. Brett isn't quite sure what it is. She listens hard as her fingers firmly grasp the flashlight that she has next to her.

Brett can hear the harsh, rhythmic breathing of Grandpa Jake. He is close by, but she cannot make out his form. Brett can also hear the soft breaths coming from Natalie and Dr. Brown. She points the face of the flashlight away from her companions and flips the switch. The bright-white beam breaks through the darkness but does not travel far. She can see about twenty feet ahead of her, and she moves the beam from left to right. Her heart starts to beat faster as the light brings the thing hiding in the darkness into view.

She doesn't want to see what could be in the darkness ready to attack, and she doesn't want to see what evil object her mind has created in the New Mexico night. As the beam falls on the shadows all around her, she begins to feel foolish. She has imagined some entity that seeks to harm her out here away from everyone. Logically, the team are the only people in this canyon tonight. She closes her eyes and tries to remember what she has heard to startle her so, but try as she might, the thought doesn't come to her. Satisfied that there isn't anything out in the darkness, she turns the light off and lies back down.

Brett looks up at the absolutely black sky. There isn't light from the moon or any stars visible in the air. The wispy dark clouds have devoured the lights from the heavens, creating a blank black canvas in the sky. Brett enjoys stargazing. She knows the locations of some of the constellations: Libra, Sagittarius, Gemini, and Leo. She has spent many nights with her dad, scanning the skies back in Camden as a Royals game played on the radio. He would quiz her and delighted in her mastery of star locations. He has always told her that the skies are essential and that they have vital information for explorers. The arrangement of the stars helps to understand how to locate points in space and time, and they also tell us about the mysteries of earth. He has always preached that the ancient peoples of North America, Meso America, South America, Asia, and the Middle East all understood the intricacies of the heavens and earth—how they relate to each other and how they generate powers that we can't fully understand.

He has said many times that modern man, in his arrogance, has forgotten what learned civilizations have passed down because modern man has a vain and proud spirit. Brett remembers the description in the field book about the Hopi and the Zuni—how they believed that there are other realms besides this one, where people can travel and confer with their gods or elders. She remembers the Mayan and Incan people's belief that the afterlife is a simple trip through a river of enlightenment.

Brett quotes the book in her head as she stares up at the dark, blank sky. Dad has collected all this information to find what the ancient peoples discovered. He has always listened. A smile flashes across her face. *She* is listening. She is listening to the ancient peoples who left detailed instructions on how to find their most fabulous treasures. She feels more connected to the past and its complexities than before. She feels more connected to the earth, its secrets, and the ancient people who built the city of Cibola.

This is what discovery is all about: the realization that people who came before you knew things that you didn't, and you are rediscovering some lost philosophy or idea of theirs. Brett can feel her heart beating faster and faster in her chest. This is why her dad listened to the Royals game the day before he went missing. To calm him, keep him focused.

Right at this very moment, her dad is sitting in one of the cities of gold. He is learning at the feet of the gods or elders or whoever they are, and she is confident that he is relishing the moment. The realization strikes her firmly that she will also be interacting with the same elders tomorrow. Her mind races as she thinks about what she will say, what questions she will ask.

The excitement begins building in her like the power of a wave during a hurricane. There is no going back to sleep tonight. She is content with that. She wishes that she could venture out now for the city, but the gateway will not open until ten or eleven. That is the hour that she and Dr. Brown have calculated anyway.

She is still on her back, looking up at the dark sky. She drums her fingers on her chest as she imagines what the city of gold will look like. She remembers the sight of its golden walls a few months ago. It has appeared that the structures are lined with sheets of gold that reflect the rays from the sun and transmit a beam of glorious golden light. The pathways that cut through the elaborate structures also emit an opulent glow, she believes. She can see herself traveling down the city streets and her dad sitting on the golden steps that lead up to the main building in the square.

She runs up the steps and throws her arms around his neck. He hugs her tightly and utters absolutely perfect words: "You have done well. You solved a mystery that only three people have been able to solve." Dr. Wilson speaks proudly, and she steps back, looking into his face. His smile is broad, and his blue eyes dance as he stares at her.

Suddenly a noise pierces the stillness of the night. Brett jumps, and the images that she is seeing disappear from her mind. Grandpa Jake lets out a billowing snore that reverberates through the canyon. Brett closes her eyes and waits impatiently for the first rays of sunlight.

*****

Daylight comes much quicker than Brett has been thinking it would. The golden rays begin flowing like cascading droplets down the canyon walls until they splatter in prism patterns on the rocky bottom. She hops out of her sleeping bag and grabs her backpack. She quickly takes out the magnetoscope and begins testing the settings. A muffled humming sound comes out of the metallic machine.

The sound grows louder, and the other members of the party begin stirring in their bags. Brett glances over at Natalie as she rolls over onto her side and opens her eyes. She wipes the rest of the sleep away and, realizing that it is morning, pulls herself out of her sleeping bag quickly. She looks at Brett and notices the device in her hands. "Today's the day," Natalie says. "Today's the day!" She jumps up and rolls up her sleeping bag quickly, then stores it in her pack. She slings the bag over her shoulder and looks at everyone else impatiently. "Mom, get up. Today is the day." Dr. Brown opens her eyes. She slowly crawls out of her bag. "You guys could show a little life this morning," she says.

Brett laughs as she turns her focus back to the magnetoscope. She turns the tuning control dial, and the humming coming from the machine slows and then stops. "All set," she says.

Grandpa Jake rubs the white stubble on his chin that tells that he hasn't had a proper shave in a few days. He opens his bags and fishes out four protein bars, passing them to each member of the group. Natalie looks at the food as if she is being asked to eat a piece of wood. Jake picks up on her view of the bar. "Celebratory dinner," he says. "Not breakfast."

Brett opens the protein bar and makes quick work of it. She has the whole thing devoured in seconds, then stuffs the wrapper in the side pocket of her cargo pants. She takes the field book out of her bag and holds it in her right hand, with the magnetoscope in her left. She looks at each of them and then checks her watch. "Six o'clock," she says. "Time to move out."

"This is so exciting," Natalie says as she walks down the rocky canyon toward the northwest.

"You think we will find it?" Dr. Brown asks as she passes by Brett.

"If our calculations are right," Brett responds.

"They're right!" Natalie yells.

"Absolutely," Brett says confidently.

Brett holds the magnetoscope out in front of her as she follows behind Dr. Brown. Grandpa Jake strolls up to her and smiles. "I believe," he says.

Brett smiles back. Those words build her confidence. She is sure that she will find Cibola, but hearing Jake talk about believing in the lost city ratchets up the intensity of her spirit. "Thanks, Grandpa," she says.

They walk in silence over the pebbles that have deposited themselves over countless years. The stones began their journey at the top of the cliff and, because of water or gravity, have found their way into the meandering canyon below. Brett has her eyes fixed ahead of her. She does not want to miss the appearance of the golden walls of a city that she is sure will appear in the distance. Brett is expecting them to emerge out of the heat bands of the hot August morning of New Mexico. She is confident that the first alert will be the magnetoscope, and it will give her plenty of warning for the appearance of the city.

They walk another hour through the narrow passes of the tall canyon. The sun starts tracing higher into the sky, and the shadows at the bottom are beginning to disappear. The heat inside the canyon continues to mount as the sunlight reflects off the orange-and-yellow stones, directing the rays toward the group as they walk onward. The sweat is pouring out of Brett as she steps over a large boulder in the path.

She checks her watch, and it is now nine in the morning. They have been walking in a northwesterly direction for the last three hours. Their pace has decreased since the first hour, and the thought of finding Cibola quickly has now eroded into the belief that maybe they were wrong.

Dr. Brown checks her map and grimaces. "Should have found it by now," she says. She looks back at Brett. "Any reading on that machine?"

Brett shakes her head. "Nothing."

Dr. Brown looks down at the map and traces their route with her finger. "I think we missed the doorway," she says.

Brett opens the field book and checks her map. Their current location is beyond the red X that she has drawn on the yellowed page. Brett bites her lip and looks ahead of her. She is searching for the heat bands that will tell her the city is near. Brett looks down at the magnetoscope and shakes the device, hoping that jostling the internal components will make it work. She adjusts the sensitivity setting, and the slow humming sound flows from the device. "It works," Natalie says. Brett switches the device off test mode and turns in circles, trying to pick up a signal. The humming stops.

Brett's heart sinks into the bottom of her stomach. She can't believe it. To be this close and not be able to locate Cibola presses on her mind and body. Her shoulders slump downward, and her eyes fill with tears. She has led them off course. The weight of failure presses on her chest like a giant rock. It restricts her breathing. *What are we going to do now?* There is no way of finding a magnetic anomaly that shifts regularly without a little help.

Brett looks up, and Grandpa Jake is staring at the ground, moving a pebble with his boots. She can see the disappointment on his face. He has been reluctant in his support of the expedition at the beginning, but the closer they come to finding the city—finding her dad—the more excited he has become. She hates seeing the distressed lines on his face appear even more distressed. She bites her lip and looks over at Natalie.

Natalie shrugs her shoulders. "It's all right, Brett," Natalie says. "We will just wander around aimlessly until it goes off again."

Brett shakes her head.

"Maybe we will get lucky," Natalie continues.

"This is the end of the line," Dr. Brown says. "We should have found it by now."

"I know," Brett says robotically.

"What if we just continue down this path?" Natalie asks.

"I don't think so," Brett responds.

Dr. Brown walks over to Brett and places a hand on her shoulder, giving her the we've-done-all-that-we-can-do look. Brett knows it is over. There isn't any way to find a magnetic field when you are in the wrong spot. Dejected, Brett looks up at the sky, trying to find an answer written in the wispy clouds that migrate through the deep-blue expanse. No answer emerges from the sky's depths. She slaps her leg with the field book and walks on down the path.

The air has become stagnant and hot. There isn't a breeze blowing in the canyon. It feels like a furnace, with the immense dry heat creating a suffocating environment which she now occupies. Every step she takes seems to increase the temperature and pressure present in the canyon. The orange walls seem to press closer toward her, creating added pressure that shouldn't be there.

Natalie and Dr. Brown watch as she walks away down the trail. "Where is she going?" Natalie asks.

Dr. Brown puts her arm around her daughter and pulls her close. "She needs a few minutes. We're going to give her that before we get out of this place."

Brett is forty yards from the rest of the group, and she continues walking. She doesn't know why she keeps going. It could be that having something to do suppresses the thought of not finding her dad. The entire time he has been gone, she has focused her mind on locating him. Now she doesn't know if she will ever find him. Esteban, de Niza, Coronado, and Rock Wilson all found the doorway. Unfortunately, Brett Wilson seems to have struck out.

She grips the field book firmly in her right hand and walks a few more steps. This truly is the end of the line. She looks back, and Grandpa Jake, Natalie, and Dr. Brown are watching her. She has moved fifty yards from them. "This is far enough," she says to herself. She takes one more step, and suddenly the magnetoscope starts chirping. She looks down at the machine in her left hand, and the red light begins pulsing.

Her heart begins pounding harshly in her chest as the chirping sound coming from the device starts to grow louder and louder. She looks back at the others, her eyes wide.

Natalie starts racing toward her. "It works! It works! It works!" she yells.

Dr. Brown follows, and Grandpa Jake laughs as he hobbles toward her.

Brett takes a step forward, and the humming sound builds and fills the canyon with a deafening roar. The sound emanating from the magnetoscope is just like it was the day she saw the walls of Cibola shimmering through the haze. Her breath comes in quick gasps as she fights to contain her excitement. Her heart continues to hammer harshly against her ribcage, and at any moment, she expects her heart to fly out of her chest.

Brett takes more steps down the trail, and the sound inside the canyon builds and builds until the vibrations begin hurting her ears, causing her eyes to water. Natalie and Dr. Brown have their hands over their ears, protecting them from the building crescendo of sound. Brett gasps as she looks ahead of her. There in the haze of heat stands the vertical golden walls of the city. The sunlight glints off the façade in gold and yellow bands, creating a glowing citadel. Her breath catches in her chest as she points to the city walls.

"Oh my!" Dr. Brown exclaims.

"We found it!" Natalie screams over the vibrant humming.

Brett steps forward absently as she gazes intently on the glistening golden walls. She has found it after all, and now she will be reunited with the person who started this quest. It will be so wonderful to see his face! She is sure that he will be proud of her for finding the city— for finding him. The disappointment is gone now, and the excitement builds into overabundant exuberance.

She takes a few more steps forward. She is within ten or fifteen yards of the doorway—she is sure of that. It is time to enter the shining city on the hill and see what it has hidden all these years. As she turns and looks back at the others, she sees a flash of silver. The sunlight reflects boldly off a figure on a horse that is galloping swiftly at them. "Oh no!" Brett exclaims as the horseman races toward them with such speed and anger she is sure his intentions are not right.

CHAPTER 12

The Noble Sentry

Brett yells loudly, and her voice is drowned out by the intense humming sound coming from her magnetoscope. She tries to alert the others by yelling. The yelling isn't working, so Brett tries a new tactic. She points toward the charging rider, and Natalie finally turns. Seeing the menacing newcomer, she shrieks and grabs her mother's arm.

Dr. Brown wheels around, and as she catches sight of the rider, she grabs Natalie and begins running with all her strength toward Brett. Grandpa Jake runs quickly for an old man, and his legs fly up behind him as he runs away from the rider.

Brett turns and points to the golden city that is radiating light all through the canyon floor. "We can make it!"

The rider is wearing armor like a conquistador, with his silver helmet and breastplate glinting in the sunlight, charging harder and harder toward them as they begin running again toward the golden city walls. Brett glances back as she stumbles over the uneven ground. She can see the flaring nostrils of the white horse the man is riding. The man's dark eyes narrow as he pulls his sword from its sheath and twirls it over his head.

"This is going from bad to worse!" Natalie yells.

"Keep running!" Brett replies. "We just need to make it to the city walls. Maybe someone inside will help us."

"I'm not hopeful!" Natalie yells back.

The man on the horse thunders toward them. He is close enough now that they can feel the pounding of the hooves through the ground. Brett glances over her shoulder, and she can see the man's black beard blowing in the turbulent air. She puts her head down and runs faster, but it is no use. The rider will overtake them before they make it to Cibola. She thinks quickly, deciding that she will stop and try her best to get in the horseman's way. If she does that, then maybe Natalie, Dr. Brown, and Grandpa Jake can escape.

Brett stops and wheels around quickly, facing the charging white stallion. There is foam spewing from its mouth as it bears down on her. The face of the rider hasn't changed, and his dark eyes appear to look right through her. Brett stands firmly in place. The others haven't noticed that she has stopped. That comforts her. She doesn't want any of them helping her.

The horse is bounding toward her. Her mind races, wondering what she should do next. She looks around, searching for something to throw at the silver-plated rider. The only thing she can use as a weapon is her pack. She quickly takes it off her back and holds it tightly in her hands. She is only going to have one shot at hitting this Coronado look-a-like.

"Come on," Brett says, "just a little closer." She can feel the hoof beats of the horse as it runs. The sweat builds on her brow and slowly trickles down her face.

"A little closer," Brett says. Her hands are trembling as she grips the bag and finally lets it fly. The pack soars through the air and bounces off the rider's breastplate. It is like a fly hitting a truck. The pack does nothing to the armored rider. The rider drives his horse toward her. Brett throws herself toward the canyon wall as the rider continues on by her. Lying on the ground, she turns and watches the horse continue toward her friends. "He's going to catch them," she says, and she jumps to her feet and runs headlong as fast as her feet will go toward the golden city.

As she runs, she sees a striking image. Ten people are running toward Natalie, Dr. Brown, and Grandpa Jake. Her friends are between the rider and the ten people, like an object in a vice. There is nothing

Brett can do but watch helplessly as they get closer and closer. Then, to her surprise, the rider gallops by Natalie and Dr. Brown and rushes forcefully into the midst of a group of men. The men scatter as the horseman chases them with his sword drawn.

Brett makes it to the spot where Grandpa Jake has stopped. He has his hands on his knees, and he is trying to catch his breath. The sound inside the canyon is now at a deafening level. Between the painful humming sound and the pounding of the horse hooves, Brett can hardly communicate with Grandpa Jake, Natalie, or Dr. Brown. Brett watches as Coronado chases the men away from the shining city.

Natalie steps over and places her mouth right next to her ear. "I think he's on our side!" she yells.

Brett nods and points toward the city. Natalie nods, and as they start toward the golden gates, three of the men step up and stand in between them and the city. Finally, Brett gets a good look at the group. She recognizes the man who is standing in the center of the group. He has a sneer on his face as he steps forward. "I knew you would lead us to Cibola, you foolish child," Dr. Sims says with a laugh.

Brett grits her teeth. She can't believe that Dr. Sims is standing in front of her. She can't believe that he is going to be the one who keeps her from entering Cibola. She can't believe that Sims is going to win.

She looks around for the horseman, but he has gone. "You see," Dr. Sims snidely says, "I am much better at discovery than you or your father." His eyes move from Brett to Dr. Brown. "By the way, Dr. Brown," he sneers, "you are relieved of your duties at the university. You're fired." He lets out a high-pitched laugh as he finishes his statement.

Dr. Brown glares at him with penetrating eyes. "You won't get away with this," she replies.

"My dear, I have already, as you say, gotten away with this," he says mockingly.

"Why?" Brett asks as her voice rises.

"First of all, your father is a nuisance," he says, laughing. "Second, I just really don't like him—or you, for that matter. So taking the discovery of the city from both of you will be delightful."

Brett looks around her for something—anything—that she can use against Sims and the members of his party. The two men standing on his right and left side are fit, and they look like military types. They have muscular arms that bulge out from their shirts. They are both wearing dark sunglasses that shield their eyes. Their faces have blank expressions, as it appears they have a job to do and nothing will keep them from completing it.

Brett tries hard to think of something to get her and the others out of this situation. If she doesn't think of something, Dr. Sims will walk into the city and claim it for himself. He truly is a selfish and devious man. He is going to tarnish Cibola. Brett can't let that happen. She isn't going to let him win. She will fight to protect the city.

"How did you find us?" she asks, hoping that keeping him talking will keep him from entering the golden city.

The smile that spreads across his face is more sneer than a smile. "Oh, my dear, you led us right to it," he says with a laugh. The humming sound coming from the electroscope is increasing in intensity. The sound hurts her ears as Sims yells so that everyone can hear him.

"You see, foolish girl. You made it so easy to follow you. You solved the riddle in your little book, and you found the way to use the machine," Dr. Sims says with a grimace. You led us right to it."

Brett stares down at the machine as it transmits the vibrant humming sound. She is disgusted with herself for leading them right to the spot where it would be. She is angry with herself that she did not think they would follow her. She felt that she had outsmarted them, but in reality, *they* outsmarted *her*.

"My plan worked perfectly," he continues."

"Why did you want the book?" she responds.

"I didn't. It was a way to lead us here," he says with a sly grin spreading across his face.

"I see why my dad said you were a poor scientist," she says.

"Don't be too hard on yourself, Ms. Wilson," he says. "Rock was just as naïve as you."

"Who are you stealing this for?" Brett asks. "Since you are taking this from us, I think we have a right to know."

"You deserve nothing," he scoffs. "But I am in a jovial mood this afternoon, so I will tell you that I am taking it for myself."

"Who are these bozos?" she asks heatedly, pointing at the other men around him.

"This is the muscle from the Department of Antiquity," he replies curtly. "The military has a vast interest in magnetism and large amounts of gold."

Brett glares at the two men. Their faces are still expressionless as they stare back at her.

Dr. Brown pulls Natalie close to her. "What are you going to do with us?" she asks.

Dr. Sims turns, looking at the shimmering bands of heat that shroud the walls of the city. He motions to the two men and says something that Brett and Dr. Brown cannot hear. The humming noise that fills the valley has become a deafening roar. It is starting to sound like a jet engine.

"What are you going to do with us?" Dr. Brown yells, straining her voice.

Dr. Sims turns with a wry smile on his pointy face, looking like a cunning fox. He places his thumb against his neck and runs it across his throat in a slashing motion. "You will die!" he yells back. Dr. Sims laughs at her as he turns and begins walking toward the gates that allow entry into the city.

The two soldiers from the Department of Antiquity walk slowly toward them. Their blank expressions cause a shudder to go through Brett's body.

Grandpa Jake places his wrinkled hand on her shoulder and leans in toward her ear. "What are we going to do now?" he whispers.

A worrying thought of how to escape rushes into Brett's mind. She could hit one of them with her pack, and that might give them enough time to escape. Then the realization that she threw her backpack at the conquistador comes rushing into her mind like the wave of a tsunami.

Brett glares at the men as they move closer to her. The man on the right pulls a pistol from his belt and smiles as he nears them. Dr. Brown wraps her arms around Natalie and closes her eyes.

Brett musters all the courage she can and decides that she is going out fighting. She will scratch and claw at these men. She won't go down without taking a piece of them with her. As she sets her feet and readies herself, the humming noise that fills the canyon floor is drowned out by the loud neighing of a horse. Brett can feel the thundering strides of the majestic white beast through the soles of her boots. She quickly grabs her grandfather and falls to the ground, then rolls toward the rock face to the right.

The soldier with the gun turns, and his blank face finally shows emotion. The horror of seeing a man on horseback with a shiny breastplate and helmet wielding a sword and racing his horse toward him is too much for the soldier. His eyes are wide as the dark-haired man with the wispy beard and dark, penetrating eyes strikes him with his horse. The soldier flies through the air and lands ten feet from where the collision took place. He lies motionless in the dust and rock.

The second soldier turns and runs in the other direction, and the man on the horse watches him go. The horse snorts and stamps its feet on the canyon floor. The man looks in the direction of the city as Dr. Sims gets closer and closer. Brett watches from the ground as Dr. Sims disappears in front of her eyes. The humming that fills the canyon suddenly stops, leaving perfect silence.

She slowly gets to her feet and looks at the dark figure sitting astride a beautiful white horse. "Who are you?" she asks bravely.

The man takes off his metal helmet, revealing a mat of dark hair. He holds his helmet under his right arm and holds the reigns of his white horse in his left. His straightness up in the saddle shows the dignity and air of nobility. Could this be a Spanish conquistador from the 1500s? Could this noble rider be a sentry for the seven cities of gold? Could this be an added protection because the city has to mask its very existence?

Brett isn't quite sure, but as the man surveys her with curiosity, he finally breaks the awkward silence. "Allow me to introduce myself. I am Hernando de la Cosa. I am a one of seven men that were charged with protecting the seven cities of gold."

Brett looks at him, not truly understanding the meaning of what he is saying. Hernando, seeing her lack of understanding, speaks carefully, as if he is talking to an infant. "Our great King Charles sent us on a holy errand, one that our Lord relayed to him. Our king presented us with a mission that was of the utmost importance. We were sent halfway around the world to find and protect the routes to our Lord's lands."

Brett shakes her head, still not comprehending what the conquistador is telling her. She thinks about the words of Hernando, but they can't possibly be true. Why were Spanish soldiers being used to protect the lands of God? *That doesn't make any sense.*

Hernando continues. "Ponce de Leon found the first, De Soto found the second, and Coronado found the third. These places are magnificent." He looks at her stoically. "But Hernando has failed His Majesty. I have allowed evil men to enter the routes established for true pilgrims. Hernando has failed in the task that Coronado entrusted to him."

"Coronado gave you the job of protecting the city?" Brett asks.

"That is correct. In 1542, he left me here with a task that no one should enter. I have failed," he says.

"Wait a minute." Brett asks, "You're over five hundred years old?"

"Of course not," he says. "I am four and thirty."

"This is crazy," Brett says.

"I have failed in my task. Now, I must leave this world forever," Hernando says.

"What?" Brett responds. "Who is going to protect the entrance to the cities now?"

"That task is now left to you," Hernando replies. "You can find and enter each of the cities, just as we could. Take heart in your task. You are now the protector."

Brett shakes her head in disbelief. She can't take on this job. She can't find and protect routes into the lands of Cibola. Suddenly a white glow emerges from the air next to Hernando. He looks over at the light as it pulses in front of him. "My time in this realm is over," he says. "You must find the next route and expel the invader from the golden cities. If they are allowed to remain, the majesty of those special places will be destroyed forever." He leans down from his horse and holds out his hand. She places her hand in his. "Be of good cheer," he continues. "Do not fear, for he is with you always until the end."

Brett watches as he pulls his hand away from hers and takes the reins of his horse. He wheels the white animal around and slowly walks toward the white light. Brett is amazed as he enters the bright doorway-shaped structure and disappears inside. The light fades quickly and vanishes, leaving the valley floor in shadow once more. Brett turns and looks at Grandpa Jake. Then she looks at Dr. Brown and Natalie. They remain silent, unable to express their real thoughts about a golden city, a Spanish conquistador they conversed with, and the fact that he disappeared into a blazing white light.

The four of them stare into the area where the bright doorway has appeared and faded from existence. They are left wondering if all they have experienced is true. Brett, using logic and scientific thought, is having a particularly difficult time. How could this be? How could her dad have missed this? He had thought of everything, but he had missed this piece of vital information. Brett wishes that she could talk to him, but he is still inside the city, and that city is hidden again by the magnetic sphere that protects it. She will find it, though. She must. That thought envelopes her mind and paralyzes her. She closes her eyes and falls to the ground, and the tears of grief flow from her eyes in a continual flow.

CHAPTER 13

The Return

The words of Hernando echo in her ears as she wipes the salty tears from her face. She peers up at the spot in the canyon where the city was once visible. All that is there now are the vibrant orange rocks reflecting light into the canyon where she is sitting. Grandpa Jake stands over her, visibly agitated by the events. He holds out his wrinkled hand, and she places hers in his. He pulls her to her feet slowly and wraps his arms around her. "It will be all right," he says soothingly.

She doesn't have the strength to reply. She feels helpless because Sims has entered into the city and yet left her here outside with no way in. The tears leave streaks across her face. "I don't know what to do," she says.

Grandpa takes a few seconds to respond. "I guess we will find another entrance," he says.

Brett pulls away from him and looks into his eyes. "What?" she says.

"We will find the other entrances," he says.

"And we will protect the cities, just like Hernando," Natalie says excitedly.

Dr. Brown looks at Natalie, her eyes wide in disbelief. "We aren't—"

Natalie holds her hand up, shaking her right index finger at Dr. Brown. "We are, too," she says sternly. "Brett needs us more than ever

111

now. That guy had to leave his post because we led Sims here. That's our fault, and we need to correct that."

Dr. Brown shakes her head. "We aren't doing it anymore. We're going home," she replies.

Natalie shakes her head. "You don't have a job anymore. Sims fired you—remember that bit of information? So, you have nothing left at home," Natalie says with great passion in her voice.

"You want to search with Brett?" Dr. Brown says.

Natalie looks into her mom's eyes. "Of course." Natalie walks over to Brett and places her bruised hand on her shoulder. "We're in this to the end, Brett."

Brett smiles. It lifts her spirits immensely, having her best friend wanting to risk everything to help her.

Natalie turns and looks up at the cliff where the city has once stood. "How are we going to find it?" she asks.

Brett stares up at the cliff, and she thinks about what they should do next. The task is daunting, but she must figure out where the magnetic anomaly will appear next. If she can figure that out, she will have the location to the doorway. That will lead her to the city—and it will lead her to her father. It will also bring her face-to-face with Dr. Sims. She is looking forward to that reunion. Sims is going to get what is coming to him.

Brett picks up her bag and throws it over her shoulder. The magnetoscope and the field book are inside. She hooks her hands inside the straps and turns to Natalie. "We need to get out of here and get back to the car. Then we can work on locating where the entrance to the city will be." Brett looks over at Dr. Brown. "With your expertise, we can do this," Brett continues.

"Let's get to it, then," Dr. Brown says.

"All right!" Natalie yells, jumping up and down, unable to control her excitement.

Brett looks ahead and starts walking over the uneven ground. The pebbles on the canyon floor crunch under her feet. She turns her head, and Grandpa Jake is right behind her, with Natalie next in line and Dr.

Brown in the rear. She is happy to have them with her on the journey. Brett isn't quite sure that she can protect the mystery of the cities without them. She also isn't quite sure how to protect the cities, but she is determined to try. Brett is determined more than ever. She must find her dad. He will help her. He will give her the information that she needs to solve the problem of protecting the cities as Hernando did. Maybe he will help her protect the cities too.

She walks in the fading sunlight, and the shadows are starting to creep along the edges of the canyon. She knows they will make it out of the canyon before nightfall. They will have to stay one more night down here. That isn't a job that will be easy, but she will give it her best effort.

Brett continues walking, and she can see a body lying in the path up ahead. Hernando did his job well. He protected the entrance from all the soldiers who fought with him to enter. Brett looks down at the man as she walks up the trail. Suddenly a pale hand grabs her leg and pulls her down. She is fighting with terror in her eyes, trying to pull her leg free from the vice-like grip of the injured man. "Esteban. I must find him. He is the key," the man mumbles.

Grandpa Jake runs over and falls on the man, but the man continues fighting and mumbling, "Esteban. . .Esteban."

Finally, Brett pulls herself free from his clutches and stumbles backward. The man stops grasping for her and is calmly lying on the ground, mumbling nonsense: "Esteban. He is the key."

Natalie is standing behind Brett. "Why is he saying that?"

Brett isn't listening. Her heart is racing, and she stumbles forward toward the man. "Grandpa, get off of him!" she says.

Grandpa Jake slowly gets to his feet as Brett slides down beside the mumbling figure.

Brett touches his face. "It's okay," she says. She looks back and motions for Dr. Brown to come over. "It's Dr. Mies!" Brett says shouting.

Dr. Mies grabs her hands and looks up at her. His face is pale, and his eyes are terror-filled. "Esteban is the key. Find him. Rock needs him," Dr. Mies says.

Brett leans down. "Why?" she asks.

Dr. Mies rolls over on his side and starts shaking violently.

"Help me!" she says breathlessly.

"Rock needs help. . ." As he finishes his words, his eyes flutter closed.

"Why? What has happened?" Brett yells. She shakes Dr. Mies by the shoulders, but he doesn't move.

Natalie, Jake, and Dr. Brown are staring down at her. She looks up at them, really fearful for the first time. "How did he get here, and why didn't Dad come back?" she says.

There isn't an answer from the others. Brett looks up at them, imploring them to give her some information, but there isn't an answer. "We need to find that entrance now! It sounds like he's in lots of trouble," Brett says. She stares down at Dr. Mies, and the weight of protecting the entrances to Cibola feels like it is crashing down on her. She has to do it, but it will have to wait. Her dad needs her. He is in danger, and she is the only one who can help.

Brett looks up at the late afternoon sky. The clouds roll quickly by, and two turkey vultures catch a breeze and glide across the blue expanse of air. "I will find you, Dad," she says. She leans over Dr. Mies. "You're going back, Dr. Mies. I need you to go back." Brett sits back, staring into space, trying to calm her nerves and focus on the next task: finding Esteban.

The End